MISSING

James Duffy

A BANTAM SKYLARK BOOK ®

NEW YORK · TORONTO · LONDON · SYDNEY · AUCKLAND

RL 4, 008–012

This edition contains the complete text
of the original hardcover edition.
NOT ONE WORD HAS BEEN OMITTED.

MISSING

A Bantam Skylark Book / published by arrangement with
Charles Scribner's Sons

PRINTING HISTORY
Scribner's edition published April 1988

Skylark Books is a registered trademark of Bantam Books, a division of Bantam
Doubleday Dell Publishing Group, Inc. Registered in U.S. Patent and Trademark
Office and elsewhere.

Bantam edition / July 1989

for Amanda and Priscilla

MISSING

1

At the final bell, Kate Prescott gathered her books and tucked them into a plastic bag. There wasn't much homework tonight. Miss Harrison didn't believe in making the fifth-graders work over the weekend. But during the week, she was fierce. I'll take my math and social studies and English home, Kate thought. I'll have time to get started on next week's assignments.

Some of the kids were clustered outside talking about their plans for Saturday and Sunday. They paid no attention to Kate. She walked down Main Street past Jenny and Martha and Pat, who were crowded around the telephone by the general store. They nodded to Kate and went on giggling into the phone.

Wingate certainly wasn't much of a town compared to Manchester, but she was getting used to it. It was pretty, and the kids had started to be friendly to her this year, not like last year when they just looked at her and shook their heads, as though she was some sort of nut.

But she had to admit there really wasn't any place for kids, only the general store with its lunch counter and the town library. After school most of the kids, unless they had athletics and took the late bus, climbed into the buses that took them home if they lived more than a mile from school. The others walked straight home or hung around the general store for an hour or so.

Kate's house was just under a mile from the school. Kate knew she wouldn't take the bus no matter how far it was. Walking home, by herself or with Sandy, was the best part of the day. It was the time when she could think about things without being bothered.

As she turned down Old Winthrop Road, she took the last piece of gum from her pocket. She began to skip along the left-hand side of the road, jumping over the puddles from last night's rain. Would Jeanette be accepted into the sorority this afternoon? she wondered. Would she leave college if they didn't take her?

Her thoughts wrapped up in today's episode of "College Town," Kate was unaware of the car behind her until it pulled alongside and stopped. The window rolled down and a man's face leaned out toward her. "Want a ride, Kate? I'm going your way."

Kate shook her head and walked on, briskly now. How did the man know her name? Had she ever seen him before? Certainly it wasn't anyone she knew. She was pretty sure it wasn't anyone who lived in town. You didn't have to be in Wingate very long to learn who most of the two thousand year-round people were.

The car, black she noted, pulled up alongside again. "Your mother said I could offer you a ride if I happened to be passing by," the man said.

"My mother?" Kate stopped and asked. "You know my mother?"

"I do indeed," the stranger responded. "My wife and I eat at the Winthrop House at least once a week, usually at one of your mother's tables. She talks about you and your sister."

Kate hesitated. "I don't know," she said. "I like to walk home. It's not far from here. I'm not supposed to take rides, even from people I know."

"I understand, but I'm not really a stranger. I'm Harry Atwood. Maybe your mother mentioned my wife and me."

Kate shook her head. Before she could move on, the car eased in front of her and a car door on the other side swung open. "Get in, Kate. I'm going down the road to look at those two old trailers. I'm thinking of buying them and fixing them up to rent out in the summer. I bet you'd like to have some neighbors, wouldn't you? Get in. You can tell me more about the trailers."

Kate knew she would like to have someone, almost anyone, living next door. "I guess it's okay," she said and climbed into the car.

Mr. Atwood reached over to pull the door shut. He was a large man with, Kate decided, a sort of friendly face. He drove slowly down the road and turned up the lane. He went past Kate's driveway and parked in front of the two abandoned trailers.

"What do you think, Kate? Should I buy them?"

"Gee, I don't know," Kate replied. "The windows are broken out back. The raccoons have probably got in there. They get into everything else. There's not much left. My aunt Peggy says they might haul the trailers off for back taxes or something like that."

"They may do that. They'd probably rather sell them cheap first. I'll take a closer look one day soon. Do you want a peppermint candy?" As he turned toward her, Kate noticed the strong, sweet smell of peppermint on Mr. Atwood's breath.

"No thanks. I'll get out here and walk back to the house. I have a program in a little while that I—"

"Wait a minute, Kate," Mr. Atwood interrupted. "I need to know more about these trailers. You say there's not much inside. Here, take a candy. They're good." Mr. Atwood took a round box from the dashboard and held out a peppermint candy wrapped in foil.

She hesitated. Then she threw her gum out the window and took a piece of candy. She unwrapped it and dropped the foil out the window. It *was* good. "There's just the sink and a couple of metal bunk beds, from what Sandy and I could see. No stove or refrigerator or mattress." Kate didn't like to ruin the chances of having people next door, maybe with kids, but she had to admit the trailers were in awful shape. "Maybe they will be cheap if you want them."

Mr. Atwood was no longer looking at the trailers. He was looking at her now with a funny expression on his face. "Maybe I'd move into one myself. How would you like that, Kate?"

It sounded weird to Kate. "They're awful small, just for summer people. I have to go now, Mr. Atwood. I don't want to miss my program."

"I know you don't," the man said. "I know all about you, Kate. Maybe more than you know about yourself. I'll tell you what. Why don't you come home with me for a short visit and meet my wife? We'll tell her about the trailers. She made a big chocolate cake this morning. She's very nice. Margaret is her name. She'll like you, too."

"Some other time, Mr. Atwood. It would be real nice some other time. Sandy could come, too. But now I have to look at my program, and my sister's waiting for me." Kate lied about her sister being at home, but the smell of Mr. Atwood's peppermint breath was stronger and closer, and Kate was frightened.

"We'll bring her back a piece of cake, that's what we'll do. You'll be home in half an hour. We live just on the other side of town."

"You do not!" Kate shouted. "You don't live in town at all. I'm getting out." She pulled the door handle. The door was locked! Mr. Atwood pushed the button. Kate's window rolled up with a soft hiss. Mr. Atwood's large hand reached out. He shoved Kate to the floor.

"Get down and stay down. Don't open your mouth," he said in a strangled voice. "You do what I say, Kate, or else." The car turned and lurched over the bumpy lane to the road.

2

Sandy went up the steps into the town hall.

The big letters on the frosted glass panel read Chief of Police, Wingate, New Hampshire. Underneath, smaller letters read Malcolm Torbert. Behind the door crackled the sounds of a police radio.

Sandy paused, biting her lip in indecision. Why did Kate have to do this to her? She was tired of her sister's foolishness. For the third time in two years she had to come to Chief Torbert's office. The first time, she remembered, she had charged into the office without knocking, her heart beating wildly with fear and foreboding. Chief Torbert and his young deputy, Parker McDonald, were playing checkers on the table where the radio crackled sounds she did not understand. The second time, just about a year ago, she had stopped respectfully, less fearful than before, to knock softly on the frosted glass panel.

Today, she was more embarrassed than afraid. I'll go home and wait, she told herself. I don't care what Mom said to do, I'll go home and wait. It's only been a couple of hours. But the thought of going home down the lonely dirt road in the early shadows of a fall afternoon, to wait alone in the gathering darkness watching the streaky pictures on the old black-and-white television, to start to listen sometime after ten-thirty for the roar of Aunt Peggy's big old Lincoln when it turned into the driveway, and to hear at last her mother's key in the lock, these thoughts were more than Sandy could bear. She had to talk to Chief Torbert. She doubled her hand into a small fist and tapped on the door.

A gruff voice ordered her to come in. The chief was seated sideways at the desk, his feet resting on an overturned battered gray wastebasket. He looked at Sandy quizzically, then smiled. "Sandy," he growled, "Sandy Prescott. Back again, are you, Sandy?" He reached over to the table and turned the radio down. "Let me guess why you're here."

Sandy stared down at the worn linoleum. Why do you do this to me, Kate? she thought. She did not answer Chief Torbert. She kept looking at the floor with a silly half-smile on her face.

The chief smiled, too. "It's all right, Sandy," he said in a voice no longer gruff. "Your mother told you to come, didn't she?"

Sandy nodded. "She's worried," she murmured.

"I reckon she is," Chief Torbert said. "I'd have been worried, too, if this had happened when my kids were growing up. What's wrong with Kate, Sandy?"

"I don't know," Sandy responded. "I don't know what's with her sometimes. She's different from other kids. She's even different from Mom and me. I just don't know."

"Look, Sandy, there's not much I can do for you right now. Parker almost cut his toes off with a power mower and he'll be out for a week. The auxiliary deputy is off fishing somewhere in the Maine woods. I can put a call in to the state police. But I have to sit here and wait for emergencies."

Sandy felt helpless. "I'm sorry I bothered you, Chief Torbert. I told Mom we should wait. I'll go on home now." She turned toward the door.

"Wait a minute, Sandy. Sit down here for a bit. I haven't seen anybody all day except the town clerk, and he's as deaf as a post. Do you remember when you and your mother and Kate first moved into town? You came running into the office here to tell us Kate was missing. How old were you that summer, Sandy?"

"Ten," said Sandy, "ten in July."

"Kate turned out to be missing, that's for sure, missing for three whole days. How old was Kate then?"

"Eight. Her birthday's in July, too."

"We got the state police on the job right away. We put out all-points bulletins. We had police and volunteers searching the woods. There were divers down at the pond. We had just asked for a National Guard unit when Kate showed up. The director from Camp Wontoona brought her back."

"I know," Sandy said weakly.

"Your sister had hitched her way over to the camp in Harwood thirty miles away. She talked her way into a bunkhouse. The girls there made her a mascot and hid her for three days—I don't know how—and Kate had a fine vacation at camp until a counselor found out."

"Mom made her stay home the rest of the summer," Sandy said defensively. "She didn't have much vacation after that."

"Maybe so," said Chief Torbert, "but what about last summer?"

"She went to Albany to visit our grandmother."

"She did, Sandy, she surely did. But she forgot to tell your mother and she didn't bother to tell you, and she certainly didn't tell me," the chief laughed. "What she *did* do was take her savings, call your grandmother from the general store, and head for Norton Falls, where she caught the bus to Albany, where she convinced your grandmother it was all right for her to be. You called your mother at the restaurant and she told you to come here."

"I know, but—" Sandy interrupted.

"It's all right, Sandy Prescott, I'm not accusing you. I just think your sister Kate is a runner. We got the dogs. They led us halfway to Norton Falls before they lost the scent. It looked like Kate got picked up along the way. We put out the bulletins, then we started asking questions. After that, Kate got in the newspapers and on the television again, where your grandmother found out. She called us up and brought Kate back. Now, where do you think she went this time?"

"I don't know," Sandy said softly. "But this time I have a feeling it's different, maybe. Kate promised last year she would never do anything like that again. Kate always keeps her word. Anyway, she only took rides with women, she said."

"Maybe," Chief Torbert said. "What happened today?"

"Kate went right home after school. I stayed for soccer practice. When I got home at four, she hadn't been there. I went back to town and asked around. No one had seen her since two-thirty. I called Mom from the general store. She said . . ."

"Don't tell me. She said, 'Go see Chief Torbert.' Well, Sandy, it doesn't sound so dreadful. Kate will show up. I can't do any more than give the state police a report. Let's just wait. We both know by now Kate can look after herself. Call your mother and tell her not to worry. I realize she has to work at the restaurant and can't keep running home. She can't do any good here and you need what she earns. Maybe you should get a phone out at the house."

"We had one," Sandy explained, "but we got behind on the bills and they took it out."

"It's going to be all right, Sandy. Let's give Kate a little more time this year before we fly into action. Why don't you go home and see if she's there?"

"But—oh, forget it," Sandy said. She stood up to leave. Her shoulders sagged dejectedly.

What if her sister really is missing? Chief Torbert asked himself. Sandy Prescott was a responsible girl, he knew from experience. She looked after Kate and their home while her mother was serving tables over at the Winthrop House. She hadn't wanted to come banging on his door this afternoon and probably wouldn't have if she wasn't worried. Sandy deserved more than his cheerful encouragement. But he was tied to the office. "Sandy," he called after her, "I have an idea."

"What is it?" she asked. "I have to be getting along home. Maybe you're right, Kate may be there now."

"If she's not, Sandy, go talk to Miss Aggie Bates. She used to be a police officer down in Boston, one of the first women on the force. Tell her the whole story. See what she says."

"Miss Bates who lives on the edge of the schoolyard? That's a summer home."

"It used to be. Aggie and her husband came up here every summer for a month, but Henry died last winter and Aggie decided to retire and move in for good. She's going to be lonely for a while until she gets used to things up here. Go and talk to her. She'll be standoffish at first, that's her way, but don't let her frighten you. Before you go, let's check on Kate's description."

Chief Torbert reached into a file drawer and pulled out a folder. "Let's see: Katherine R. Prescott, Old Winthrop Road, et cetera, et cetera. No phone. Hair, light brown, curly. Eyes, blue. Freckles on nose. Height, four feet. Weight, seventy pounds. Bad scar on left knee from skating cut. Dress—what was she wearing today, Sandy?"

Sandy tried to remember. "Uh, old jeans, I think, the ones with tattered bottoms. Plaid shirt, sort of brown and green. It's one of my old ones. Tan windbreaker with patches on the sleeves. You know, ski patches, flags, racing patches. Sneakers, real dirty. And I guess you better add a couple of pounds and an inch or so. Kate has grown in the last year."

"Got it, Sandy. Anything else?"

Before Sandy could answer, a different sound came over the radio. Chief Torbert turned it up and listened. "I have to go, Sandy," he said. "A bad accident out on the highway. You talk to Aggie Bates if Kate's not home. And come see me early tomorrow. Don't worry. We'll find Kate. Or she'll find herself."

3

The sun had dropped behind the sugar maples beyond the schoolyard. Now in mid-September, they had begun to take their autumn colors. Another year, Agatha Bates sighed, but a year without Henry. She felt old and lonely sitting outside on the porch wicker rocker watching the last few children kicking a ball. She took a swallow of cold tea, gathered up her magazine and the teapot, and went inside. She shut the French door behind her to keep out the early evening chill.

What to have for supper? she wondered. With an absentminded frown, she scanned the cupboard shelves. Without thinking, she took down a can of tomato soup. Then she recalled she'd had that last evening; half a can was sitting in the refrigerator. She put the unopened tomato soup back on the shelf.

While she stood pondering in front of the open

cupboard, the thud of a soccer ball against the house shook the shutters. Enough! Agatha said to herself. Enough and more than enough! Since school started her house had become a backstop for errant soccer balls. She went out to the porch and looked over the schoolyard. No one was in sight. An old brown ball lay on the ground. Agatha was tempted to roll it back toward the goal as she had done before. No, she thought, not this time. They'll have to come and talk to me if they want it back. She carried it inside and tossed it on the sofa in the living room, startling the sleeping yellow cat. "I'm sorry, Tom," she told him. "It's suppertime anyway. Come in the kitchen and I'll feed you."

Bending over to give Tom his chopped liver, Agatha heard a soft knock at the front door. She smiled triumphantly. We'll get a few things straight once and for all, she told herself. She pulled open the door. "You want your ball back, I suppose?" she said sharply.

Sandy did not know how to respond. What was Miss Aggie talking about? "I don't want any ball, ma'am," she stammered. "Chief Torbert said I should come talk to you. Maybe it's too late. I'll come back tomorrow, if that's okay."

Agatha looked closely at the tall girl standing in front of her. Jeans like the ones all the girls in town wore, a sweatshirt, and filthy sneakers with holes in the toes. A cheap polyester jacket was tied around her waist.

"You don't want the soccer ball?" Agatha Bates snapped. "You do play soccer, don't you? I think I've seen you out on the field." Which wasn't altogether true, but as Agatha thought about it, she realized she had seen this tall, blond-headed girl charging across the field.

"Yes, ma'am, but not today. I mean, not late today. I've been down at the town hall."

"Oh, then you didn't come for the ball, after all. Well, what do you want, child? Come in, don't stand there. I can't let the cold air in the house. What's your name?"

"Sandy Prescott." She followed the gray-haired woman into the living room. "You're Miss Aggie?"

"No, I'm not Miss Aggie. That's what people in town have called me since I came here to live when my husband died. My name is Agatha Bates. You may call me Mrs. Bates or Agatha, as you choose." Her tone softened as she saw the worried, confused look on Sandy's face. "If we're going to be friends, you'd better call me Agatha. Sit down and tell me what Chief Torbert sent you over here for. Malcolm is a great meddler. He probably told you I used to be a policewoman. He also probably told you I could use some company."

Sandy nodded. She stroked the purring Tom, who had jumped into her lap and curled up. "He said you might be able to help. He's on duty all by himself." Sandy paused. "But I don't think he would have done much anyway."

"Much about what?" Agatha asked.

"My sister Kate. She's disappeared."

"That doesn't sound right. Malcolm must have had a reason for not taking it seriously. He wouldn't have sent you over here to talk to me about a missing child if he thought it was urgent. Am I right?"

"Sort of, ma'am."

"Agatha, please."

"Yes, ma'am—I mean, Agatha. You see, it's not the first time. Kate ran away two years ago and again last year. Chief Torbert thinks she's done the same thing again today and will show up when it suits her."

"I see. How old is your sister, Sandy?"

"She's ten, but she's pretty responsible for her age. We have to be," she added. "Mom works over in Winthrop until late at night."

"What do you think, Sandy? Did she run off again?"

"I don't know what to think. I went home after soccer practice and Kate wasn't there. I went down to the general store where some of the kids hang around after school. No one had seen her recently. I called Mom at the restaurant and she said to talk to the chief. Then I went home again. Kate still wasn't there, so I walked over here the way Chief Torbert said."

"She went home with a friend?" Agatha suggested.

Sandy shook her head. "We don't have any really good friends here. Mostly it's Kate and me. The other kids think we're sort of strange, especially since Kate keeps disappearing."

"The library?"

"I went by there."

"You're worried, aren't you, Sandy? Do you think Kate's going to cause you more trouble?"

"It's not that, Agatha." Sandy finally got Mrs. Bates's name out. She felt better about sitting there talking to the stern-looking old woman in her rocking chair. "I don't care much about what other kids say. I'm used to being teased. Mom says you have to make your own way in the world. Well, we can do that, Kate and I," she said defiantly.

"What is it, then, Sandy?"

"Kate's got this program on television at four o'clock. It's sort of a serial about kids in college. She's really hooked on it. She wouldn't miss it for the world. And she said . . . well, maybe she didn't mean it."

"What did she say?" Agatha persisted. "If I'm going to be of any use to you, Sandy, you have to tell me things, even if you don't want to or even if they seem unimportant."

"She said last year, after she sneaked to our grand-mother's in Albany, she would never do anything like that again. She promised Mom and she meant it. I know she did, even if Chief Torbert doesn't believe her."

"And your mother believes her?"

"She always believes us. We don't lie to her."

"But Kate did run off twice," Agatha reminded her, "without telling your mother or you. That's a dangerous thing for a young girl to do these days. What about that?"

"I don't know. It was awful, I guess, but it wasn't lying."

Agatha Bates was touched by the ferocity of Sandy's loyalty and her faith in her younger sister. She remem-bered back to her own three children, in whom Henry and she had tried to instill a fear of lying—if not a love for the truth. So far as she knew, they had never hidden things from their parents. Abruptly she stood up. "I'm going to fix us some supper. Soup and sandwiches all right with you?"

"You don't have to bother, Agatha," Sandy replied. "I'll get something at home."

"I know I don't have to bother, but I'm going to. Come sit in the kitchen and tell me everything from the beginning. Throw the cat out the door. He hasn't been outside all day."

While Agatha opened a fresh can of tomato soup and made tuna salad sandwiches, Sandy told her about Kate's two disappearances. She tried to recall as many details as she could. And she tried to keep her own reactions out of the story.

Agatha listened intently. She interrupted Sandy only twice with questions. The first was whether Kate had ever done anything like this before they moved to Wingate. The second came as a surprise to Sandy. Agatha took the last bite of her sandwich, chewed it slowly, then asked, "Sandy, how do you *really* feel about what Kate has done?"

Sandy shrugged her shoulders helplessly. "I don't know. I guess I don't like it much. Mom and I have enough problems without dealing with Kate's running off. But that doesn't mean I don't want her back. Kate's my best friend as well as my sister. I love her. Kate is something special."

"Good," said Agatha Bates. "I am going to need some help, and I've been wondering if I can count on you."

"You can count on me," Sandy promised. "I'll do whatever you want me to." She pushed her chair back. "I'll be on my way now."

"I'll take you home. I want to see where you live. Maybe Kate will be there. And put your jacket on. It's cold outside."

Agatha drove past the school and down the main street past the general store, which was still open, and the town hall.

"Go down the road toward Winthrop and turn off onto Old Winthrop Road. We live to the left about a mile down," Sandy directed.

Agatha turned left at the Prescott mailbox onto a rutted lane. A hundred yards down, her lights flashed on a mobile home in a pine grove. A yellow bulb hung over a tiny porch.

"Kate's back?" Agatha asked.

"No. I turned the light on when I left, just in case. I'll wave if she's inside." She opened the door. "Thank you very much. I'll go see Chief Torbert in the morning."

"Why don't you wait for me to come by first? I want to talk to your mother. Is she at home on Saturdays?"

"Weekends are her busiest days," said Sandy. "She has to go to work a little before eleven."

"I'll be here before then. Does anyone else live nearby?"

"Not down here. Beyond the turnaround the road is grown over. It used to be a logging road, they say. There are two trailers under the trees that belong to some summer people, but they haven't used them as long as we've been here."

Sandy ran up to the front door and went inside. She reappeared in a moment to shake her head.

"Good night, Sandy," Agatha called. "I'll see you tomorrow." She hoped that Sandy had not noticed the concern in her voice. For some reason she was fairly certain that Kate Prescott had not run off again.

4

At dawn, Tom the cat jumped down from the sofa, stretched, and padded into the kitchen. He sniffed his empty bowl and meowed. His complaints unheeded, Tom went to Agatha Bates's room. He pushed the cracked door open and leaped up onto the bed. He stretched out under her chin, purring furiously.

Agatha was dreaming of a camping trip somewhere in the West, a place with mountains and cool lakes and grassy meadows. Henry had made the fire. The boys had pitched the tents. When they sat beside the fire for supper, Sarah was not there. "Sarah, Sarah, where are you?" Agatha called. There was only an echo from across the lake. "Sarah, Sarah," she cried again. Silence. Terror struck her heart. She stumbled to her feet and took her husband's arm. "Henry, where is she, Henry?" She could scarcely breathe. She raised her hands to her throat. Agatha felt the furry Tom. She sat bolt upright, clutching the startled cat.

"Oh, it's you, Tom. I'm sorry I frightened you," Agatha mumbled. It was a bad dream. Sarah was gone. Stroking Tom's silky yellow coat, Agatha focused her mind on the real Sarah, now a mother with three children of her own in San Diego. She was safe. "I'm getting old and silly," muttered Agatha. "You left me with a lot of dreams, Henry, when all I wanted was you."

As she heated the water for instant coffee, Agatha's disjointed thoughts came to rest on Sandy and Kate Prescott. From what Sandy had told her, Agatha guessed that Kate's two disappearances had been attempts to escape from a lonely new home in a town where she had few or no friends. But that seemed behind her now. Kate was not unhappy in school. She got along with her teachers and the other fifth-graders, even if she had made no really fast friends. She had her television show and her homework. They weren't much, to be sure, but they were routine and Kate seemed secure in her daily life. She didn't run away again, Agatha was convinced. Perhaps she went off overnight with a schoolmate and Sandy didn't see her note. That was unlikely, but you could never tell.

She gave Tom a saucer of milk. She put jam on a piece of stale bread and sipped the tepid coffee. Agatha had neither slept nor eaten with any consistency since that night last winter when she had sat beside the hospital bed, listening to her husband's final choking breaths. She was just as lonely in her Wingate cottage, she realized, as Sandy and Kate were in their mobile home in the pine grove.

At the time it had seemed sensible to leave the apartment in Boston that was now too large and too expensive and move up into the white cottage where she and Henry and their children had spent, she was convinced, the best times of their lives. That was what the children said when they agreed to come and visit her regularly. They had come, of course, and she had no complaints with them. They came in the summer, each child for a short visit, and returned to their own busy lives in San Diego, New Haven, and Chicago. They all promised to be back at Thanksgiving or Christmas.

Agatha Bates snapped her thoughts to attention. Stop feeling sorry for yourself. That part of your life is over. Take hold of what you have and make sense out of it. You have a job to do now, not much of a job, maybe, but a job. Sandy and her family need help. Get busy!

Agatha threw the toast into the trash and poured the coffee down the sink. She found the box of oatmeal and measured half a cup into boiling water. She made some strong tea in the cracked brown pot. There, she thought, as she sat down at the kitchen table again. There, it's a beginning.

In the back of the closet, Agatha found a pair of white sneakers she had bought years ago and had never worn. She turned her nose up at their newness. They would never do. She took them to the edge of the garden and rubbed dark loam into the canvas. She surveyed herself in the closet mirror: dirty sneakers, rolled up jeans, bulky sweater. I've joined the gang, she thought. Just *which* gang, she wasn't sure. She paused for a moment. She went to the corner table and took a black case from the drawer. You could never tell, maybe her old badge and I.D. would come in handy. She stuffed the case in her hip pocket.

Winthrop Road, really Old Winthrop Road since Route 219 had been extended twelve miles to the highway in Winthrop, cut off to the left from 219 at the edge of town just past the United Church. It was a wide dirt road with a sort of path along the right side that hikers used. Not many cars went down the road except in July and August when the summer people came to Wingate. Going to Winthrop, they preferred the picturesque dirt road with its stretches of sugar maples and falling stone walls. The regular inhabitants preferred Route 219. There were not many year-round houses on Old Winthrop Road, and for the rest of the year traffic was light.

Walking down the path toward Sandy's house, Agatha noticed erratic footsteps on the other side of the road. A long step and a scuffing short step with the left foot. Then a long step and a scuffing short step with the right foot. Curious, she crossed the road. She put her foot in the prints and tried to walk. Of course, she thought, someone was skipping along here, facing traffic the way she was supposed to. It must have been Kate. Thursday night it had rained hard. Footprints and tire marks were pressed firmly in the damp dirt.

Agatha Bates followed the skipping footsteps. Down the road, halfway to the Prescott house, the skipping stopped and two feet turned at an angle toward the road. Then the tracks continued, no skipping this time, just regular measured strides. Agatha went back to where Kate, if it was Kate, had stopped. Tire marks curved from the right over to the left side of the road. They continued on the left. About fifty paces farther on, the footprints stopped and turned out again. They went to the middle of the road and disappeared. The car tracks swung back to the right side of the road.

Intent now on following the heavy, wide indentations, blurred in places by the marks of other tires, Agatha turned into the rutted lane where Sandy lived. She passed the driveway to the mobile home. The wide tracks went farther down to where the trailers perched beneath the pine trees. There the car had made a wide turn and headed out the lane. The tires had cut into the ground at the beginning of the turn, scattering dirt and gravel. Someone had left in a hurry. Agatha could find no fresh footprints in the area.

I'll get Malcolm Torbert out here this morning, she said to herself. I'm no Indian tracker. Maybe a mother of a school friend came by and picked Kate up and took her to their home for supper. Maybe. More likely, maybe not. She noted that car tracks up the driveway to the mobile home did not resemble the heavy markings she had been following.

Sandy and a tall, good-looking woman met her at the

door. Sandy's mother said, "I'm Lydia Prescott." Her smile was tired. Lines of worry had begun to form beneath her blue eyes. She poured Agatha a cup of coffee and offered her a stool at the counter.

"Kate didn't come home?" Agatha Bates asked.

Sandy and her mother shook their heads.

"You didn't find a note anywhere, perhaps in her room?" Agatha asked.

"She didn't come home," Sandy said. "I can tell. Her books aren't here. Her bed isn't made. The first thing Kate does when she comes home after school is make her bed. She went somewhere after school."

Agatha turned her stool to Lydia Prescott. "Do you have any idea where she could have gone? A relative's house? Sandy mentioned an Aunt Peggy. Other relatives?"

"None. None at all. And no friends except for Peggy." A few tears ran down her cheeks. "I feel so guilty, Mrs. Bates. Kate knows I have to work to keep us going, but she still needs a mother for more time than I can give her. I only see my girls for an hour or two in the morning. My sister takes me to Winthrop at ten and I can't get back until after ten at night when the restaurant closes. I take my afternoon break at Peggy's place. It's just down the street from the Winthrop House."

"And your husband—I assume you are divorced. Would Kate go to him?"

"We're separated, Mrs. Bates. Ralph had his problems. The children and I couldn't deal with them anymore. We just left. Peggy took us in. She got me the job at the Winthrop House where she works and lent me the money to put down on the home. We haven't heard from Ralph since we left two years ago. I guess he's still over in Manchester."

"You don't think Kate has heard from him?"

Lydia Prescott wiped her eyes. "I don't think so. He meant a lot to Kate. She was his girl, sort of. She still talks about her dad more than Sandy here does. I know she's hurt he hasn't kept in touch. But I don't think she would dare go back to him. She certainly didn't try to reach him when she left before."

Agatha could see no point for the moment in pursuing the matter of Ralph Prescott. The story had a dreary familiarity. She was sure she could find out more from Malcolm Torbert. "And Peggy would have brought Kate back last night or this morning if she had shown up there late at night?" It was a useless question, Agatha realized, but she tried to make Lydia Prescott fix her attention on Kate's absence.

"Of course. Kate's all right, Mrs. Bates. I know she is. That's what I keep telling Sandy. It's not her fault. Kate's looking for something. She's out there trying to find it. We'll just have to wait until she checks in."

Poor woman, she's protecting herself, Agatha thought. Otherwise, she'll go to pieces. There was no point now in telling Sandy and her mother about the tire tracks. She needed to discuss these with Malcolm. "Are you playing soccer today?" she asked Sandy.

"Just a pickup game this morning with the Upton juniors."

"I'll be there to watch, part of the time anyway. My kids never played soccer. It will be my first game. Good-bye, Mrs. Prescott. I'll go have a talk with Chief Torbert now. We know Kate can look after herself. There's no point in staying here. Sandy says Saturday is your busy day. You'll be better off working. We'll get in touch with you right away if it's important. I can drive Sandy over to Winthrop."

5

Malcolm Torbert listened carefully to Agatha Bates. From time to time he asked a question. When she had finished, he sat up straight in his wooden desk chair and said, "I reckon I'd better go have a look. I'm not much of a tracker, Miss Aggie, but I grew up in the country and I can tell a tire track from a footprint."

"Malcolm, you've called me Miss Aggie for some reason since I came to Wingate last spring to live. I am a widow, not an old maid. I would like you to call me Agatha or, if you want to be professional, Lieutenant Bates."

Chief Torbert laughed. "What kind of an officer were you, Agatha? In all the time I've known you and Henry, I never asked."

"Not much of any kind, just a regular police officer who worked her way up to lieutenant and didn't get any farther. I was a teacher for six years after I left college. I didn't like that so I changed jobs. I was on the police force for thirty years and quit when Henry got sick. That was five years ago. It was a man's world. I never did much real detective work, if that's what you are trying to find out."

"I read about the woman on the ledge you talked back into the hotel room."

"That was my only famous case. The poor thing wanted to talk to a woman, and I was the only one around. Now, what about Kate Prescott? Are you going to sit there all day chewing gum or can we go out and look at the tracks?"

"I suppose I can leave the office for half an hour. Do you have your car outside or do I have to spend taxpayers' money on another wild goose Kate chase?"

"You look as though a walk would do you good, Malcolm. There's no point in living in the country if you don't get out and enjoy it."

Chief Torbert laughed again. "You got out of bed on the wrong side this morning, didn't you, Agatha? We'll take the cruiser. I can't leave here for long."

Agatha gritted her teeth in exasperation. She was going to have difficulty convincing the chief of police that a missing Kate was serious business, no matter that the child had a history of running away. She hoped the car tracks would convince him that Kate was carried off.

From the side of the road she watched Malcolm Torbert bend over, then squat to examine the path of

Kate's footprints. He walked slowly to where the car tracks swerved over to Kate's side. He went on to the point where the steps came to an end and the car went over to its proper side of the road.

"The car stopped twice, then whoever it was got into the car," he informed Agatha.

"That seems pretty clear. But you mean Kate, don't you, Malcolm?" Agatha asked.

"I have no evidence it was Kate. It could have been anyone with a smallish foot."

The chief was being ornery. Agatha refused to be baited; she said nothing. She watched again from under a pine tree as he studied the car tracks in front of the trailers. He followed them carefully as they circled toward Old Winthrop Road. Then he walked back toward the cruiser. His eye caught a flash of silver. He bent down and picked up a piece of foil. Next to it was a wad of gum. He picked that up also and put it on the open palm of his hand, which he held out to show Agatha Bates.

"The car was parked here a little longer than down on the road, I think. I'm pretty sure it's a heavy car, something like a Buick or Lincoln. Someone threw out a piece of gum. Probably the same person then ate a piece of candy." He lifted the foil to his nose. "Peppermint candy," he declared.

"What do you make of it, Malcolm?" Agatha asked quietly. She did not want to antagonize him.

Chief Torbert was equally careful. He did not want to

offend Agatha, who was his friend and in a way a fellow police officer. It looked as though Kate—it had to be Kate; no other kid lived down the road—had talked to someone she knew, was tempted to take a ride, refused, changed her mind, and got in the car. The driver—some kid's mother, almost certainly—came down here to turn around and stopped to look at those two old trailers. They were sort of a curiosity in town. Some kid—a friend of Kate's, almost certainly—gave Kate a peppermint candy. Kate went on home with them, maybe for supper, and decided to spend the night.

He explained this to Agatha, who, as he feared, did not agree.

"Kate would have left a message," she objected. "And her precious television show, she wouldn't have missed that! And what about right here where the car accelerated? Someone was in a hurry." She pointed with the toe of her sneaker to the scattered dirt and gravel.

"Well, the way I figure it, it was all right to go visit. From what you tell me, no one had ever asked Kate before. She could look at her program wherever it was she was going. She would come home later. No need to leave a note. She could explain to Sandy later. Then the other kid asked her to spend the night, and that was pretty nice, too, to have a sleepover. She told her friend it would be okay with Lydia. Kate can be pretty persuasive, I can tell you."

What Malcolm said made a kind of sense to Agatha. Kids weren't all that responsible when it came down to having a good time. Growing up, her own children had a steady stream of friends passing in and out of the apartment, raiding the refrigerator, hogging the television, rocking the walls with loud music, spending the night whenever they wanted. She couldn't remember that she or Henry had ever once asked if that was all right with the parents, though she realized now they should have.

"What about these?" she asked, pointing to the skid marks again.

"The driver gave it too much gas. It happens to all of us. Look, Agatha, does anything else make any sense? No other footprints, here or down on the road. No sign of any struggle. If someone had taken Kate, was he—or she—going to park down a dead-end road next to her house? The candy wrapper and the gum, they look pretty normal to me. I tell you, Kate will show up this afternoon. It's happened twice before."

"I hope so," Agatha said doubtfully.

"If she doesn't, I'll go into action. I've already notified the state police to be on the lookout. Parker may be able to come in and help. 'Course I'll end up looking foolish like before, but that's part of the job."

Agatha was not altogether satisfied with Malcolm's explanations, but all she could do was poke around until tomorrow. As she got out of the cruiser, she asked, "Could I have the candy wrapper, Malcolm?"

"Going to work, are you, Agatha?" Chief Torbert handed her the silver foil. "Good luck. Let me know when Kate checks in."

6

The man who called himself Harry Atwood hesitated as he came to Old Winthrop Road. Then he turned the car sharply to the left and sped toward Winthrop. "What have I done?" he muttered. "What have I done? All I wanted was to drive around for a little while with Kate and talk with her. I wanted to be her friend. But now I'm a kidnapper. I can't explain this to the police." He realized he was speeding. Terrified, he slowed the car. In the mirror he peered behind him. The road was empty.

His impulse was to pull over to the side and tell Kate Prescott to get out. She could walk home from here. He would ask her not to tell anyone about what had happened. He would give her a handful of the candy. Maybe she would keep quiet. But maybe she wouldn't.

What would he do then? he asked himself. She could tell the police enough for them to find out who he was.

He had no reason to suppose she was stupid. If he put her out, she would look at his license plate and remember the number. That would never do. In his mind's eye, Harry Atwood saw himself with his hands chained at his waist being led into custody. Photographers and television people were recording his disgrace. He was suddenly cold inside. His hands were sweaty on the steering wheel. Sharp pains cut through his chest.

He went slower. He took peppermint candies from the box on the dash. With trembling fingers he unwrapped one and put it in his mouth. The other he extended down to Kate. She did not take it.

Somewhere, I'll find a quiet place, he told himself, and we'll talk. I'll explain to her what happened. She'll understand, I'm sure she will. I'll tell her it was a mistake and take her back to Wingate. Once I explain, it will be all right. We'll be friends, just the way I wanted us to be. "You'll be all right, Kate," he said out loud. "Just stay down there a little longer. Then we'll have a good talk." At the sound of his voice, Harry Atwood felt a sense of relief. Kate would understand.

There was no response. "Kate," he said in a louder voice. "Did you hear me, Kate?"

Kate did not answer. Was she all right? Had he hurt her? Or was it all a dream? he wondered. Maybe it never happened. Was this something he was imagining? Was there someone really down there on the floor? He reached his hand down to his right. He touched a sneaker. It was jerked away. He was not dreaming. Kate

Prescott was huddled out of sight on the floor of his car. Terror surged inside his body.

By now he had come to the center of Winthrop. Winthrop House appeared on his right, set back from the road on the crest of a sloping lawn. He would stop and Kate would run inside to her mother. She wouldn't pay any attention to the license plate when she saw where she was. Her mother wouldn't want to make any trouble, Harry Atwood told himself. Then he would go on home. No one would ever know. And if they did, he'd say Kate Prescott was hitching a ride and he took her over to Winthrop. They were bound to believe him.

And if they didn't, he'd still have time to get away. He imagined the police officer getting out of his cruiser and going to the front of the house. He knocked at the door. Inside, Harry threw some clothes into a bag. He ran down the back steps and raced off in his big black Buick past the startled officer. No one would ever find him. After a while they would forget and he could come home again and everything would be all right.

He snapped to attention. He was well past the Winthrop House headed out of town on the highway to Manchester. Why was he on this road, which led him back toward his house? Well, let the car decide his fate. Harry Atwood slumped back against the seat and followed the white line on the highway. He was exhausted, his head empty of plans and imaginings. Whatever happened would happen. Things were beyond his control. He would go wherever the Buick led him.

All the while Kate sat hunched on the floor. How long had they been riding? She had recognized the bumps of Old Winthrop Road. They were going to Winthrop. But from there, she could not be certain. Her legs were getting stiff. She knew if she didn't move them soon, she would not be able to run if she had a chance. Somehow she had to stop the car. She could be sick, she thought. She spoke for the first time. "Please, sir, I think I'm going to be sick. I don't feel well. Could we stop, please?"

The voice seemed to come to Harry Atwood from a great distance. But it was a voice. It was Kate's voice. She had spoken to him. He could be her friend after all. Now they could go home and talk. It was going to be all right.

He answered cheerfully, "Just a little while, Kate, and we'll get out. There's no place to stop along this road. Stay down there for fifteen minutes, then we'll be home."

That trick didn't work, Kate thought. Her legs were about paralyzed and her neck was stiff. Carefully she rubbed her legs and turned her head from side to side. Mr. Atwood had said they'd be home soon. Did he mean her home? Had he decided to take her back to Wingate? By now she had missed her program, she was sure of that.

Although she was still frightened, Kate was no longer terrified. She had a kind of feeling that Mr. Atwood was not a regular criminal, like the ones she saw on television. He was well dressed and he had tried to be friendly. He knew her mother, or so he said. The thing to do was not to get scared so that she couldn't take care of herself. That's what they told her on the program about missing kids. Just keep cool, they said. If you scream and cry, that upsets people. Kate rubbed her legs and waited.

There is nothing else to do now, Harry Atwood concluded, but take Kate Prescott home. Then he could decide. There was plenty of time. No one was likely to be looking for her down a lonely country road thirty miles from Wingate. When he came to the cutoff for Madison, he left the highway. Slowly he settled back into the familiar routine of his existence. He paused at the flashing yellow light in Madison center, waved to Natalie Grover, who was coming out of the post office, and drove carefully out of town.

Home for Harry Atwood was a large fieldstone summer house that had passed through many careless hands for sixty years before it came into his possession. The sugar maples that used to line the lane up to the house were dying. Brush from the neglected fields and orchards had pushed to the edge of the driveway. The lawn was overgrown with weeds. The veranda around the front of the house sagged on rotting beams.

Harry Atwood drove to the rear and parked by the back door. The garage beyond the house was filled with furniture and yard tools and two cars resting on flat tires.

Atwood got out and opened the door for Kate. "Well, here we are," he announced. He took the house keys from his pocket and tossed them lightly in his hands. "Stretch your legs and come in. Be careful of the second step. The board is loose."

He unlocked the door and held it open for the stumbling Kate. He reached inside to switch on the lights. "Wipe your feet on the mat, Kate. I like to keep the floor clean," he instructed.

Kate looked around the big old-fashioned kitchen. She had never seen a room quite like this one, not even on television. The walls were shining white. That black iron contraption must be an old wood stove. Next to it a refrigerator with a sort of an enameled beehive on top. Across the room, a big wall of counters and glass-doored cupboards. Another wall of gray stone sinks. On the floor black-and-white linoleum, worn to the boards in places, but polished to a dazzling gloss. In the middle of the room sat a heavy, square wooden table with a single wooden chair and a single place mat.

She saw Mr. Atwood watching her with a kind of friendly smile. He was waiting for her to say something. "It's awfully big," Kate said. "It's nice and clean, too," she added. She looked around again. "Is that where you eat?" she asked. "How come there's only one chair?"

Mr. Atwood kept on smiling. "You're right, Kate," he said. "We'll have to get another chair for you."

Kate felt the same sudden fear she had felt when Mr. Atwood pushed her hard to the floor of his car and beat it down the road. She realized that something was very wrong. "What about Mrs. Atwood?" she demanded. "Where's her chair?"

Still smiling, Mr. Atwood said softly, "There's no Mrs. Atwood here. There's just you and me, Kate."

7

By the time Agatha Bates reached the playing field the soccer game was almost over. The Wingate team was wearing yellow jerseys. Agatha watched Sandy race across the field to keep the ball in bounds. She kicked it toward a teammate, but a girl in a blue jersey intercepted it. The referee waved her arms. Each team gathered to shout a brief cheer for the other team. The yellow jerseys headed for the general store; the blue jerseys climbed into cars, which turned down the road toward Upton.

"Who won?" Agatha asked Sandy.

"No one. It was sort of a tie. They brought only eight kids, so we played only eight. We agreed we wouldn't keep score. What did Chief Torbert say, Agatha?"

"Come along to the house and we'll have some ginger ale," Agatha responded. "I'll make you a peanut-butter sandwich. It's about all I have until I do a big shopping over in Winthrop. I try not to eat lunch. Then I'll drive you home and we'll see if Kate has shown up. The chief thinks she'll make her way back today from a friend's house."

"Kate didn't spend the night with a friend. She doesn't know anyone that well. My mother wants to think maybe that's what happened, but she doesn't believe it either. I guess she really thinks Kate ran off again. I just don't know. I have a feeling something awful has happened. I just hope she'll be home and we won't have to worry about her for a while."

Kate was not home. Sandy told Agatha she would have turned the yellow light off. She reached inside the cinderblock step for the key. She shouted halfheartedly for Kate, then went down to her sister's room. She returned shaking her head.

Agatha did not want to frighten Sandy Prescott, but there was no point in not sharing her fears. Perhaps Sandy knew something that was important without realizing it. "I don't want to upset you, Sandy, but I don't altogether agree with Chief Torbert. I think Kate went off with someone, yes, but someone who might not be a school friend." She told Sandy about the tire tracks and the signs that a car had parked down at the end of the lane by the trailers.

"Malcolm says it must have been a mother who pulled down there to turn around and stopped for a moment. I don't buy that. You can turn around easy enough down at the beginning of your lane. I'd guess it was someone else, perhaps someone Kate knew—or even knew about. She wasn't forced into the car, and anyone who meant her harm wasn't going to park on a dead-end road just beyond her house. Tell me, Sandy, is there much traffic down your road here, like hunters or kids who want a place to drink beer or even strangers who get lost? Are there people who want to walk in the woods?"

"Not since we've been here," Sandy answered. "Every once in a while at night some kids tear down to the end and then back to Old Winthrop Road blowing their horns and shouting. But not recently. The woods aren't much for walking. There's poison ivy down the old road and the mosquitoes are fierce until the first frost. They shoot pheasant over on the other side of the woods in back of the trailers, where the ball field used to be. There aren't many people in Wingate and there are lots of other places for them to go, down to the pond or the town forest or the activities field."

"Chief Torbert found this," Agatha said. She showed Sandy the peppermint tinfoil. "Have you seen this kind of wrapper before?"

Sandy shook her head.

"And he found a piece of gum. I don't have that."

"Blue?" Sandy asked.

Agatha tried to remember. "It may have been, but I can't be certain."

"If it was blue it was Kate's. She's weird about bubble gums. This month she's only chewing blueberry bubble gum. In October, she says she'll switch to cinnamon.

Here, I'll show you." She reached under the counter and showed Agatha a coffee can half filled with bubble gum. She unwrapped one. "This is blueberry."

"That's something to tell Chief Torbert," Agatha said.

"Could I see the tracks, please?" Sandy requested. "You're sure they're not my aunt Peggy's?"

"They're not like the tracks that go up to your house. There's not much tread left on those tires."

"Aunt Peggy keeps saying she's going to get new tires, but she never gets around to it. She better do it before the snow comes, or she won't get up the driveway."

Sandy and Agatha walked down to the turnaround. Agatha showed Sandy the tracks and the place where the mystery car stopped and where Malcolm found the gum and the candy wrapper. "The other tracks are the chief's car."

Sandy squinted at the ground. "There aren't any others, are there? I told you it was lonely out here. We live on the empty side of Wingate, my mother says. Most everyone lives on the other side, toward the pond and the old mill. Which way did the car go when it got to the road?"

Agatha was startled by the question. Neither Malcolm Torbert nor she had thought of that. They had got in the cruiser and gone back to the center. "I don't know," she said, embarrassed. "We better go see."

There were two sets of tracks turning left from the lane onto Old Winthrop Road. "Those are my aunt's," Sandy pointed down, "and here are the other car's. They're headed to Winthrop."

"Who lives down the road for the next couple of miles?" Agatha wanted to know. "I can't remember when Henry and I last took this road over to Winthrop. The new road is so much quicker."

"Well, there's the Campbell place about half a mile down. It's a big old farmhouse; you can't see it from the road. They didn't come up this summer; at least, I didn't see their car. About a mile up on the left is the Perkins place. They were here all summer—they have a Jeep. Up beyond there's a road into the hills to a couple of shacks. I don't know those people. After that you're in Winthrop. It's pretty empty all along the road until you get close to Winthrop center."

"Let's walk down the road to the Campbells'," Agatha suggested, "just to be sure the car didn't turn around there."

They picked out the familiar treads along the road, sometimes obscured by the treads of other cars that had passed their way.

"The Campbells' lane is up there by the dead elm. Do you think someone went up there?"

"We'll see. Where does that go?" Agatha pointed to a dirt track through the bushes on the left.

"That goes back to the old ball field. It's getting to be all grown up. There must be some pheasant there. We hear the shooting during the season. People used to dump their trash there, but not anymore. Kate and I used to poke around in there for junk when we first moved."

Agatha Bates paused, indecisive, for a moment. Sandy had said that the field lay in back of the trailers beyond a strip of woods. "Let's poke around there ourselves for a minute," she said to Sandy. "Then we'll go down to the Campbells'. After that we'll go see Chief Torbert."

The old ball field had become a deserted meadow. Saplings, sumac and pine, were rising above the tall grass. The frame of the backstop still stood, but the wire was gone. Along what had been the right field base line a car path stretched toward the woods. In places the path was bare. Agatha bent over a patch of dirt. The rain had not altogether washed away the tire tracks.

"Someone has been back here not too long ago, wouldn't you say, Sandy?"

Sandy knelt beside her. "Gee, I guess so. You can't tell much from these. They're all mashed."

"Yes," Agatha agreed, "but let's see where they go."

They followed the flattened grass to the edge of the woods where the car tracks ended.

"There's a path over to the trailers from here that Kate and I used to take. Come on, I'll hold the branches back for you." She strode ahead, holding back the bramble vines and low pine branches for Agatha to pass.

Suddenly, she bent over. "Look, Agatha," she shouted. She held out a silver foil wrapper. "It's like the one you have, isn't it?"

Agatha took the tinfoil from her pocket. Sandy smoothed both out in her hand. They were identical.

"Let's keep going, Sandy," Agatha said. She swatted at the mosquitoes attacking the back of her neck.

They crossed the pine-needled yard from the woods to the trailer nearest to the mobile home. Sandy reached up and pulled the handle of a metal door. It opened easily and quietly. Sandy stepped up and put her hand down to Agatha. Together they looked around the empty trailer. The floor beneath the counter in the tiny kitchen was littered with familiar candy wrappers. Agatha rubbed her fingers over the counter top. They came away clean—no dust, no dirt. She reached across and turned the handle of the louvered window. The glass strips opened to give Agatha a perfect view of the Prescotts' little home.

"Someone sat here on the counter," she mused, "eating peppermint candy and watching your place from the window. The door has been oiled, the window has been oiled. From the number of wrappers, I'd say he or she has been watching for a good while. Did you ever sense you were being watched, Sandy?"

Sandy shook her head.

"Well, whoever it was knows where your sister is right now, I'll bet my life on it. We better talk to Chief Torbert right away."

8

"Hi, Sandy. And how are you, Miss Aggie?" Parker McDonald greeted them. Chief Torbert's deputy sat in Torbert's chair. His foot, thickly bound with bandages, rested on the chief's overturned wastebasket. "I hear your sister Kate has disappeared again," he said to Sandy. "Don't you worry, she'll be back."

Agatha resisted the temptation to tell the young deputy the next time he called her Miss Aggie, she would kick the wastebasket out from under his injured foot. She asked as calmly as she could for the whereabouts of Chief Torbert. Malcolm, she and Sandy were informed, was having a cup of coffee at the general store.

"How's your foot, Parker?" Sandy asked kindly. She was fond of the deputy, who had worked around the clock two years ago looking for Kate. Last year when

Kate ran off to her grandmother's, Parker had been equally kind to her mother and her.

"I lost parts of a couple of toes, Sandy. My own dumb fault for sticking them under a power mower, but I didn't need them anyway. I'm not going to enter the Olympics this year. Doctor Cheever says I can put my shoes back on in a week or two. Are you worried about Kate? She'll be all right. She has a way of looking after herself."

During the exchange, Agatha Bates fidgeted. It was important that the search for Kate begin as soon as possible. "Sandy, could you run down to the general store and tell Chief Torbert we'd like to talk to him? And while you're there why don't you look at the boxes of candy on the shelf?"

Sandy, puzzled at first, was about to ask Agatha what she wanted, when she realized what she was being asked to do. She made a circle of understanding with her thumb and middle finger and hurried out of the station.

"Well, what have you got, Agatha?" Malcolm Torbert stood in the doorway. "You didn't even give me time to finish my coffee. Sandy said you two had made a discovery, didn't say what it was. What have you been up to since this morning? I gather Kate Prescott hasn't come home yet. The state police reported in a while back. They haven't seen anyone like Kate hitching or walking along the roads. I tell you, Agatha, be patient. Kate will be back before the weekend's over. Isn't that right, Parker?"

"I hope so, Malcolm. The Prescotts don't need any more trouble."

Sandy ran into the room. She nodded yes to Agatha.

"Good," said Agatha. "Now we know a little more, perhaps. While Chief Torbert and I go to the trailers, could you go back to the general store and see if anyone there remembers who buys these mints and how many boxes they sell in a month, and anything else about the mints that you can find out. We'll return in a little while."

Turning to the puzzled chief of police, she said, "Let me drive you over to the trailers in my Toyota and save the taxpayers' money. There's something there I'd like you to see. If I'm right, you and Parker are going to have a busy weekend."

Going up the Prescotts' lane, Agatha stopped at the mobile home and banged on the door. Satisfied that Kate had not come home, she drove down to the turnaround. She led Chief Torbert around to the rear of the first trailer.

"You open the door, Malcolm," she instructed. "Notice that the hinges are oiled so that the metal doesn't squeak. Then give me a hand up. My back's getting a little stiff with all this running around."

Inside the trailer, Agatha pointed to the kitchen. She showed him the foil wrappers on the floor. She took from her pocket the one the chief had given her that morning.

"Also notice there's no dust on the counter in there. It's been washed clean, I think. The window handle has been oiled. Try it. The window faces the Prescott place. What do you make of it?"

Chief Torbert did not answer immediately. He turned the handle and peered through the open louvers. He bent over to pick up the peppermint wrappers. He laid them out, one by one, on the counter and studied them. "Well, I suppose I could say that the Prescott kids had been playing a game here in the trailer—a kind of secret game kids sometimes play in deserted places—but I don't think you'd buy that, would you, Agatha?"

"I came here with Sandy, Malcolm. I saw her reaction. I didn't bother to ask her anything like that. Look at the rest of the place. No one's been in there for years. Would you like to see some car tracks on the other side of the woods?"

"On the old ball field, down the car path hunters use?"

Agatha nodded. "They aren't clear because of the rain and the grass that's matted down, but I'll bet anything they'll match the ones out front here."

"So you sent Sandy to the general store to find out about the peppermints, did you, Agatha? That's police business now, not stuff for kids to mess around in."

"I'm glad you recognize your responsibilities, Malcolm. It *is* police business. But kids can help, too. We can all help. You're the one who put Sandy off on me. She can find out just as much in the general store as you or Parker. Now, tell me what you think."

"I think Kate probably isn't visiting a friend, just what you thought this morning—with no evidence whatsoever, I remind you. Anything more I can't tell you. You're saying someone has been watching the Prescott place, probably Kate, for a good while, that someone talked her into a car, parked out front for a moment, then took her away—or persuaded her to go off. Is that right?"

"Yes. The car turned toward Winthrop when it left the lane. That may be important, too, though I don't know why. Kate's in trouble, Malcolm, you can be sure of that. People who do things like this aren't always responsible for their actions."

Chief Torbert remembered the earlier investigations into Kate's runaways. Both times he had feared, until Kate showed up, the worst. He had done the obvious thing first. He had satisfied himself that she had not gone to visit her father in Manchester. Lydia Prescott had implied that her husband had a drinking problem and had been violent at times. Torbert had asked the police in Manchester to check up on Kate's father, who still had, he was informed, the problem. They were sure Kate had not come that way. Now could it be that their father had been watching his children? Kate was apparently his favorite. Had he talked Kate into going off with him? He would call Manchester as soon as he returned to the office.

"Maybe the father," he said hesitantly to Agatha Bates. "It doesn't seem likely to me but you never know."

"Kate would not have done such a thing to her mother, not without leaving a note. If she ran away before, it's because she was unhappy in a new place. She didn't go to Manchester then, and she didn't go off with her father yesterday."

"She may not have had a chance to leave a note," Torbert argued. "The car left in a hurry. Parents kidnap their own children sometimes, Agatha. You must know more about that than I do. We live pretty quiet lives here in Wingate."

"That may be a reasonable assumption, Malcolm, but does the rest of it fit? Can you see him sitting in a trailer eating candy and watching his daughter? I can see him better driving up when Lydia is off at work and trying to be friends with the girls again. Lydia said he liked Sandy and Kate. They were deeply hurt he didn't stay in touch."

Chief Torbert told Agatha he could find out about Mr. Prescott soon enough. He would ask the state people for help at once. They would look for fingerprints, but that never seemed to work out. The prints were always too smudged or incomplete or something else. If Kate had actually gone off with someone who had been watching her—and there was more evidence now that she did rather than didn't—she was in trouble. Did that person just get tired of watching or did he discover something that led him to talk to Kate directly?

He expressed his doubts to Agatha as she drove him into town. "I can't understand it," she said, "I simply can't understand it. But we better hurry up. I'm not sure what happened yesterday was meant to happen. If that's so, Kate is in real danger. That's what you have to deal with, Malcolm."

Sandy was waiting for them. "It's French candy.

They've been carrying it for over a year. That's what Mr. Reed said. Mrs. Reed wasn't there. Her husband said she'll know about who buys it, since she's at the counter more than he is. She'll be there later on. Of course," Sandy added, "I've been thinking we don't know the candy was bought at the general store, do we, Agatha?"

"No, we don't, Sandy. We have to start somewhere. We'll talk with Mrs. Reed later if Chief Torbert says it's all right. He's going to ask for detectives from the state police. Kate may have made a bad mistake when she got in that car. Why don't you and I drive over to the Winthrop House to fetch your mother? You and she can stay in my place until we find Kate. It's closer to town and I have a phone."

"Don't worry, Sandy," Parker spoke up. "Tell your mother not to worry too much. Kate knows how to take care of herself. We'll get her back this time, too."

9

The sign at the bottom of the lawn told Agatha that the Winthrop House had been an inn since 1780. It was a large, square, white building, a brick chimney rising from each corner.

She parked in the graveled lot beyond the house. At four-thirty in the afternoon, the lot was half filled with cars, expensive foreign models, many of them with out of state plates.

"Your mother works in a fancy place, Sandy," Agatha observed. "I don't think Henry and I ever ate here. You and I look a little scruffy in our jeans. Do you think we should use the back door?"

"I don't know. I've never been here before. My mother says they're sort of particular about things. It's hard for her to use the phone. I have to call her at Aunt

Peggy's during the after-lunch break. On Saturdays and Sundays she works straight through."

I'm too old to creep around to the service door, Agatha thought. She took Sandy by the arm and led her into the reception room. Elegant was the word for the Winthrop House: Oriental carpets, heavy silk drapes, colonial antiques, a curving staircase up to the second floor.

A tall, gray-haired woman approached them.

"We'd like to speak to Mrs. Prescott, please." Agatha spoke to the woman's questioning look.

"Mrs. Prescott? Is she having tea, do you know? I don't believe we have a Mrs. Prescott registered."

"Lydia Prescott," Sandy spoke up bravely. "She works here. She is my mother, and we have to talk to her."

"Ah, Lydia, you mean. I'm afraid she's on duty now. I believe she will break for a few minutes in half an hour or so. Perhaps you could return then. There is a staff entrance at the back of the parking lot."

Enough of this silliness, Agatha said to herself. She took a small black case from her pocket and snapped it open to reveal her badge and identification to the startled woman. "I am a police officer. We can't wait. Please bring Mrs. Prescott here now. The matter is urgent."

The woman flushed red. She opened her mouth to protest, thought better of it, and disappeared down a hallway. Lydia Prescott came into the room about a minute later. She looked upset.

"Hello, Mrs. Bates. I'm sorry if you had trouble with

Mrs. Meredith. We're not supposed to have visitors, at least not out front here. Is something wrong? Is it Kate?"

"Yes, Mrs. Prescott, I'm afraid it is. Why don't you get your things and come with us. You might want to tell your Mrs. Meredith you probably won't be in tomorrow."

"What has happened to Kate?" Lydia Prescott blurted when they were outside. "She hasn't come home, has she? She wasn't spending the night with a friend after all?"

Agatha explained that Kate had disappeared. They had good reason to believe that she had gone off yesterday afternoon in a car with someone she knew or someone she had no reason to distrust. She described their discovery of the candy in the trailer and how Chief Torbert and she suspected that someone had been watching their house for months perhaps, they could not be sure how long. Chief Torbert was calling in the state police to help in the investigation.

"Kate would not have gone off with someone she didn't know," Lydia insisted. "When she was hitching rides, she only rode with women. After the last time she took a vow she'd never get in a car with a stranger again, man or woman. She would have kept her word."

"That's what I said, Mom," Sandy commented. "You have to believe that, Agatha."

"No one dragged her into the car," Agatha pointed out. "She hesitated, apparently, maybe even refused. Then a hundred feet down the road, she got in. Why?

Who was it? I doubt that it was a friend. Do you have any idea, Lydia? Your husband? Malcolm Torbert is checking that out."

"No. If Ralph wanted to see them after all this time, he'd do it right. He certainly wouldn't carry one of the girls off. He doesn't have a car, so far as I know, and he doesn't have a driver's license. I can't remember that he used to eat candy."

"Cars, Lydia? I'm sorry. May I call you Lydia? You can call me Agatha. It will be easier for both of us. Have you seen any cars down your lane or the same car passing up and down Old Winthrop Road? A heavy car, I think."

Lydia Prescott shook her head. "I'm only home on Mondays and Thursdays, but I haven't noticed anything out of the ordinary since we moved in. The girls know more about what goes on around the place than I do."

Agatha had not expected anything else. She told Lydia Prescott she would like them both to stay in the cottage with her until Kate was found. "I have lots of room, and we can't be running all over the place. In cases like this it's mostly a question of sitting and waiting.

"And, Sandy, I have a job for you. Will you make a list of the teachers at the school and their phone numbers? And another list of Kate's friends, the ones she was closest to. We'll start calling when I get back from Chief Torbert's. I'll stop in at the general store and talk to Mrs. Reed."

Mrs. Reed was behind the counter making change for a teenager. "Here you are, Wilson, five dollars in quarters, just what you asked for."

While she waited, Agatha located the mints on the candy shelf. They were in a round silver box with the Eiffel Tower on top. They were expensive, three dollars for half a pound. She took them to the counter.

"Hello, Mrs. Bates. You're interested in these candies, too, are you? My husband said Sandy Prescott was asking about them. They're quite good. I take a box home every once in a while."

"Does anyone else buy them regularly?" Agatha inquired.

"That's what Sandy asked Mr. Reed. Are you two working together on a project?"

"Something like that," Agatha replied. "It would be helpful if you could remember."

"Oh, I can remember things all right. I told Mr. Reed the mints were too expensive to sell here except to the summer folks. We sell a box every once in a while, but nothing regular if that's what you mean. It's not worth carrying them."

"Not many town people buy them, Mrs. Reed?" Agatha sympathized. "How about this past summer? You don't recall a stranger who might have stopped in a couple of times?"

Mrs. Reed looked sharply at Agatha Bates. "You *are* after something, aren't you, Mrs. Bates? There was this man who bought the mints, maybe three or four times over the summer. I don't know who he was. He didn't dress like the summer people, in shorts and alligator shirts and funny hats, things like that, you know. He wore a proper suit and shirt and tie. A dark sort of winter suit. I suppose you'd like to know what he looked like?"

"It would help me," Agatha replied.

"He was pleasant enough, nice smile. Tall man, middle-aged, getting a little fat. Glasses, he wore glasses, with a thin rim or no rim at all. He wouldn't talk much. I tried. I'm pretty good at getting people to talk. I like to find out who people are if I don't know them. Are you still working for the police down in Boston? People said you'd retired since your husband died."

"I have retired, Mrs. Reed. This is another matter. I don't think the man will be back, but if he should come in, try to catch his license number and call Chief Torbert. I don't suppose you saw his car?"

"It's something serious, isn't it? You don't have to answer," Mrs. Reed said. "No, I didn't see his car. I'm sorry to be asking too many questions about your business, but gossip is about all we do in Wingate. Do you want to buy the mints?"

Agatha gave Mrs. Reed three dollars. She left her car in front of the general store and walked over to the police station. Now she knew a little more. The stranger—if it was the same person—was a man, and he had been watching Kate during the summer. If he had been from the vicinity Mrs. Reed would have known him, Agatha was certain of that.

A state police car was parked at the station. Inside, the trooper was talking seriously with Malcolm and Parker.

"Hello, Agatha," Chief Torbert said. "I was telling

Lieutenant Sansone here about you. This is Agatha Bates, Lieutenant. Agatha, this is Vincent Sansone. He's going to help us."

Agatha told them what Mrs. Reed had remembered.

"That's something," Malcolm said. "I knew it. I figured it wasn't anyone from around here. She took a ride from a man, did she? Sandy told me Kate only took rides from women."

"She told me the same thing, and her mother said she promised never to hitch again. I tend to believe Kate kept her word, or tried to. She must have had a good reason to take that ride. The man knew about her, didn't he? He had watched her, knew what she wore, how she acted, what her life was like, and he must have seen a lot of Lydia and Sandy."

"He must have felt like a member of the family by the end of the summer," Lieutenant Sansone went on. "Then Kate went back to school. He probably was lonely with nothing to do, so he decided to meet Kate. I think we have a nut on our hands, Torbert. We better get busy."

10

Kate was hungry; scared, too, but mostly hungry. The kitchen didn't look like the place where she was going to get any chocolate cake, especially since there wasn't any Margaret in the house. Mr. Atwood still stood quietly in the middle watching her with a creepy smile on his face. Actually, it wasn't so creepy. It was just that it didn't change. She might as well ask for the cake anyway. She would settle for a bowl of cereal or some peanut butter and crackers.

"I'd like that chocolate cake you promised me, Mr. Atwood. I always have a snack when I get home after school."

"I know you do, Kate. You go right into the house and have a snack while you look at your program, don't you? You don't go outside until later."

Kate looked at him suspiciously. "How do you know so much about what I do?"

"Oh, I have my ways, Kate. I have my ways. You told me you had to get home for your program, didn't you?"

"What about my cake?" Kate repeated.

"I don't have any cake in the house. I don't eat sweets—I mean, except for peppermints. Do you want one of those?"

"I'd rather have something to eat if it's all right with you," Kate said.

Harry Atwood went to the wall of cupboards. He had not opened some of them, it occurred to him, in a long time, not since Sharon and then Margaret had gone. He ate on the road almost always, except for breakfast, which never changed—a soft-boiled egg, a piece of wheat bread, and tea. What a stupid thing to do, he thought, to bring Kate here before he was ready for her. Kids ate a lot, most of it junk food, he supposed, but if that's what Kate wanted, he should have had it. There was nothing on these ancient shelves he could offer her.

"What did you have in mind, Kate? I haven't done any shopping for a couple of weeks."

"I don't know. It doesn't matter much. I'm just hungry." It was clear to her that Mr. Atwood didn't know his way around in his own kitchen. She might as well look for herself. If she could find something and eat it, then maybe he would be satisfied and take her home. It didn't have to be chocolate cake. That was Mr. Atwood's idea.

"Let me look," she said, as she moved between Mr. Atwood and the open cupboard. She peered at the cans and boxes on the shelf. Oatmeal, ugh. Canned beets, salmon, coffee. Where was all the good stuff you found on kitchen shelves, stuff people wouldn't let you have? It looked as though someone had used up everything you liked and left the rest. She shoved the cans to one side. In the back, her eyes caught sight of a familiar green label. Pineapple! That would do. She grabbed the can, wiped the dust off with her hand, and gave it to Mr. Atwood.

"Pineapple would be fine. Could you open it, please?"

Happy that he could offer Kate something, Mr. Atwood took the can. He reached into a drawer where the can opener should be. He could not find it. Something is wrong with me today, Harry Atwood thought. He shoved aside the jumble of knives and spatulas and ladles and all the junk he never used. Where was that green-handled opener? He pushed to the back of the drawer. There in the corner was a rusty old-fashioned can opener, the kind his mother had used, the kind with the corkscrew tucked in the handle. He managed to puncture the can and begin awkwardly to cut open the top. Halfway around, his hand slipped and his finger ran across the jagged edge of the top. Mr. Atwood sucked in a swear word. Without looking at the finger, which he suspected was bleeding badly, he hurried to one of the sinks and ran water over the wound. The sight of blood made him dizzy. He took a white handkerchief from his pocket and wrapped it around the finger.

Kate picked up the can. She found a fork in another drawer and pried up the lid. She poked the fork inside and pulled out a slice of pineapple.

"I'll get you a saucer, Kate. Just a minute," Mr. Atwood protested.

"Don't bother, sir. This is fine," Kate told him. She took another slice of pineapple. After eating a third slice, Kate pushed the lid down and took the can to the refrigerator. There was nothing inside but a carton of eggs and half a loaf of bread. It wouldn't take you long to starve to death in this house. She turned to Mr. Atwood, who was unwrapping the handkerchief.

"Well, I'm ready," she said cheerfully.

"Ready? Ready for what, Kate?"

"Ready to go home. I've had my snack and"—Kate had an inspiration—"I'll be on my way. I can get home by myself. I'll get my bearings and hitch back to Wingate. I'm pretty good at getting rides. Thanks for the visit. It was great. I'd like to come back sometime and bring Sandy." She turned to the door. She took the handle and pulled. It did not open.

"The door is locked, Kate. I know that you can probably find your way home. But aren't you better at finding your way away from home? It's almost dark now. It will be better if I take you home," he paused, "when we get around to it."

Harry Atwood looked out the windows over the sinks. It was almost dark. The shadows obscured the lane stretching away from the house. In his mind's eye he saw

Kate walking bravely down the lane toward the town road. But, suddenly, it wasn't Kate. It was another child, someone who looked like Kate, in another time, walking bravely down the lane to meet the bus. Kate's voice, louder than before, broke into the confusion. What was she saying?

"When are we going to get around to it?" Kate asked. "If I'm not home by suppertime, my mother will be worried. So will Sandy. Let's go, Mr. Atwood."

"Your mother won't be home until her usual time," he answered. "But Sandy will be worried. It's too bad you can't call her up and explain that you'll be late."

Kate's suspicions and fears deepened. How come Mr. Atwood knew everything about her and her family? "Look, if I'm not home when Sandy gets there, she'll go to the police."

Mr. Atwood's smile returned, but it was not reassuring. "So she may, you're right. I don't think the chief is going to do much of anything, not at once, anyway. He's been stung twice, hasn't he, Kate? I'm counting on that. We need some time to talk, you and I."

"I don't think I'm going to talk any more with you until you take me home," Kate threatened, trying to sound determined. "There's nothing to talk about. I don't know you, and I don't believe you know my mother."

"But I do, Kate, indeed I do. I guess I stretched the truth a little bit. She doesn't know me, at least not to talk to. I have eaten at the Winthrop House at a table where she served me. You look like her, Kate, more than Sandy does. Does Sandy favor your father?"

No answer from Kate. She stood, small, frightened, but resolute, next to the door. She didn't understand what Mr. Atwood was getting at, but she was done with playing games with him. If she didn't say anything, and he got all talked out, maybe he'd take her home. On "College Town," when Professor Harvey's young second wife got mad and didn't speak to her husband, he ended up doing whatever it was Judy wanted. Kate thought he was kind of dumb to give in so easy.

"Aren't you surprised I'm telling you so much about yourself?" Harry Atwood asked.

No answer from Kate.

"You can't figure it out?" he teased. "You're a television star. Twice I've seen your picture—not a very good one now that I've seen you in person—in the last two years, when you went off to Camp Wontoona and last year when you decided to visit your grandmother. I have your picture in my scrapbook in the study. I'll show you later on. And Sandy's picture and your mother's. You could almost say I've been collecting you, the way people collect movie stars and ballplayers. It was about time I met you in person."

Kate was curious. Why should anyone want to collect her? She bit her lip and said nothing.

"I liked you, Kate, from the time I saw you on the television. You reminded me of someone. Sometimes I even thought you might be that someone. After a while I decided I'd have a better look, so I started visiting the old trailer next to your house early in the summer. When business brought me that way in the afternoon I'd come through the woods once or twice a week to see what you were up to. I began to get fond of you. Didn't you ever feel in the back of your neck that someone was watching you?"

Kate opened her mouth in surprise. Mr. Atwood had no business spying on her. She tried to remember what she had said or done that she shouldn't have. She couldn't remember anything, but she felt embarrassed all the same.

Mr. Atwood seemed to pay no attention to her surprise. He kept on talking. He was saying something about wanting to meet his TV star personally, wanting to talk to her. It didn't make any sense. Maybe she better find out what he was trying to say. It was really weird.

"Why did you have to carry me here, wherever here is?" she shouted. "We could have talked at the turn-around, and I wouldn't have missed my program."

"That's what I thought, too, Kate, I honestly did. But I hadn't finished talking when you tried to leave the car, and I got excited and made a mistake carrying you off. Now I'm not sure it was a mistake. I think it was meant to be this way. It's right that you should be here."

"Why?" screamed Kate. "What's right about it? It's not right at all. I don't live here. I live at home."

Harry Atwood had his smile on again, a soft, anxious smile. "No, Kate, you're wrong. You're right in this house. I can feel it and I can see it. I think this will be your home."

11

Sandy and her mother had completed the list of Kate's classmates when Agatha Bates returned. Agatha suggested that Lydia begin calling the parents and asking them to talk to their children. She knew from her experiences that it was often helpful to the family in trouble to be included in what was going on. Malcolm might not approve, but she would worry about that later. While Lydia was on the phone, she and Sandy would prepare a pickup supper.

"What shall I say to them, Mrs. Bates? I've never done anything like this before. I don't know any of these people."

"Tell them that Kate has disappeared, that Chief Torbert has reason to believe she didn't run off this time. Then ask if it's all right if you talk to their son or daughter to find out if Kate said anything to them about a secret friend or going off to a special place. Parents sometimes pick up their children at school. Ask them if they have noticed anything out of the ordinary at pickup time, a stranger or an unfamiliar car. The man we are looking for hasn't made any great effort to hide his presence. You may come across something useful."

"I'm so embarrassed, Agatha. This is the third time Kate has brought attention to us."

"You must understand, Lydia, that Kate did not run away yesterday. She was carried away, probably without her consent, but we cannot be sure. Make the calls. After the first one, it will be easy. You'll find that everyone will be very kind. I'll get you a notebook from my desk. Sandy, you can help in the kitchen."

Sandy hugged her mother and followed Agatha into the kitchen. Agatha told her to shut the door; it would be better if her mother felt no one was listening. Then they discussed what the makeshift supper could be and decided on an omelette, which Sandy would make, and a salad of garden lettuce and the last tomatoes of the season, which Agatha would make.

As they settled around the table, Lydia Prescott announced she had only two more calls. Agatha had been right, everyone *was* extremely kind. "I don't feel like so much of a stranger any longer," she told Sandy and Agatha. "They all wanted to know what they could do. Some of them had helped look for her when she disappeared the last time. They said they had seen Kate on television and would keep a sharp lookout for her.

Kate is kind of a celebrity in Wingate, I guess, even if it's for the wrong reasons."

Agatha was interested in what Lydia had just said. "Kate was often in the news both times she disappeared?" she asked.

"Oh, yes, especially the first time," Lydia replied with a slight touch of pride. "There were reporters and television crews from Manchester and Portland and even one Boston station. They were parked outside our house for two days. You see, Camp Wontoona had no television sets, otherwise Kate would have been brought home right away. Last year there wasn't so much fuss, but the story was on the local news and in the papers. That's how my mother found out. Two days after Kate arrived, she saw her picture in the Albany morning paper."

"I see," Agatha said. "Well, that should help us now. Lots of people know who Kate is. Sandy and I will clean up while you finish your calls. Then I want to talk to several of Kate's teachers and the principal."

Sandy wondered why Agatha seemed so interested in the attention paid to Kate. She was a little bit jealous. At school she was sometimes referred to as Kate Prescott's sister, no matter how many goals she scored or how high on the honor roll she rose. It wasn't really Kate's fault, she supposed, but Sandy wished her sister would settle down. She didn't want to go off to the consolidated high school the year after next as Kate's older sister. She dried the last plate and put it on the shelf.

"What do you think, Sandy?" Agatha asked her. "Do

you think someone has taken an interest in your sister because he saw her on television? Things like that happen every once in a while these days, especially in my business—or what used to be my business."

"Kate is not exactly a movie star," Sandy observed tartly.

Agatha did not have a chance to reply. They heard Lydia's excited voice in the next room. Then they heard her call out, "Agatha, Agatha, I think I may have found out something."

Mrs. Sinisalo, the last number on the list, had answered the phone. Debby was visiting her cousin in Upton. When Lydia had explained the reason for the call, Mrs. Sinisalo told her that she sometimes came to the center to pick up Debby because they were on the far end of the bus route and it took Debby almost an hour to get home after school. She parked with some other mothers across the street from the school. Mrs. Sinisalo remembered that at least twice during the first week or so of classes there was a black car parked there, too. A big car, she didn't know which kind, with a man driving it. Mrs. Sinisalo knew most of the parents, and this was no one she had ever seen before. A middle-aged man, she thought, maybe wearing glasses. He seemed to be parked there, along with the other cars, waiting for school to get out. That's about all she could remember. She didn't know how long he stayed there.

"That's a lot of help," Agatha congratulated her. "This is bound to be the man at the general store. Chief

Torbert will be able to verify it from other parents. I must say," Agatha said half to herself, "the gentleman doesn't make any efforts to conceal his activities. There is almost a pattern to what he is doing. Now, Sandy, tell me who the third-grade, fourth-grade, and fifth-grade teachers are, and the name of the principal."

The teachers were all at home on a Saturday evening, which surprised Agatha, who was still used to the weekend activity in Boston, when the police had their busiest time. The three teachers spoke highly of Kate's intelligence and natural good manners. She was no problem in school; they all felt that it was the abrupt change in her family life that led Kate to run off during her first year in Wingate. They assured Agatha, especially Mary Pierce, the fifth-grade teacher, that Kate seemed to have integrated into the school community, although she still had not made any deep friendships, perhaps because of her reliance on Sandy and her uncertainty on how her schoolmates viewed her. The teachers found it hard to believe that Kate would have taken off again. They had no explanation or additional information.

The first response from Principal Peter Bouchard was the same. Yes, he knew Kate fairly well. He had talked to her regularly the last two years. Kate was unhappy when she first came to Wingate and then ashamed of what she had done. She was a good kid, just like her sister. You could count on both the Prescott girls, he assured Agatha. With a little help they would go a long way.

Agatha listened patiently. When Bouchard had finished, she gave him the details of Kate's disappearance. "Mrs. Sinisalo told Lydia Prescott an hour ago she noticed a large black car across from the school during the first week after school opened this September. It seemed out of place to her. Do you know anything about that? It is possible, though we have no evidence, that the driver may be the man who loaded Kate into his car and drove off with her."

"I'm sorry, Mrs. Bates, I don't know anything about a car. I haven't honestly noticed anything out of the ordinary. Life in Wingate is pretty quiet and routine. We're apt to notice the variations. Something a little odd happened *last year* toward the end of school. Let me see if I can get it straight."

The principal paused for a minute. "I have it now. Miss Petry—she was the school librarian and assistant secretary—took a call. It was a man who wanted to know when school let out in the afternoon. He said he might have to pick up a child while the mother was away. Miss Petry told him he had to have proper authorization and talk to me. We're very careful about these arrangements, Mrs. Bates. Apparently the man said he understood. Then he wanted to know when school vacation started. Miss Petry probably told him, but she began to be a little suspicious about the questions. When she asked the man for his name and the name of the student he was picking up, the man thanked her and hung up, without giving any answers."

"That's very helpful, Mr. Bouchard. I'm sure Chief Torbert will want to talk to you and Miss Petry. There's nothing else you can remember?"

"Chief Torbert will tell you that Miss Petry went back to North Carolina to look after her father, who is ailing. One thing more I recall now. Miss Petry said the man had a shade of a southern accent. That sort of surprised her. She hadn't heard a southern voice around here in a long time. I think I've covered everything, Mrs. Bates. Good luck and my best to Mrs. Prescott. I certainly hope you find Kate in good health."

12

Harry Atwood was exhausted. He took off his glasses and rubbed his eyes. The events of the afternoon had worn him out. He realized that his problems were only beginning. What was he going to do now that he had Kate under his care? Kids were a big responsibility, and he was not yet prepared to look after her. He should have thought of that sooner, he told himself.

There would be the matter of the police, also. Sooner or later, when she didn't show up, they would start looking for Kate. Of course they wouldn't find their way to a lonely country house thirty miles from Wingate, but it was something he would have to consider until they gave up on finding her. Technically, he supposed, he was a kidnapper, but he knew that Kate didn't think he was, and she would explain to the police in case they came this way. She would tell them he was her friend and she was just visiting and they would go away.

For the time being the question was what to do with her. He probably could not trust her until they were good friends. If he did not watch her, she might run away. After a while that would change, but right now she was like a new puppy. He would have to keep his eye on her or lock her up until she learned that this was her house. Now he had to rest or the headaches would come back. He would take care of the details later. He was good at taking care of details. When you thought about it, that had been his job most of his life—taking care of details for other people.

"Come along, Kate," he said. "It must be close to your bedtime. I'll show you where you are going to sleep."

Kate scarcely heard him. What had happened to her finally sank in. Her strength and resolve collapsed. She was trapped. Mr. Atwood had stolen her and brought her to this horrible old house and locked her up. She wasn't going to see her mother or Sandy ever again. She didn't even know where she was. She sniffled. Tears began to roll down her cheeks. Then she wept out of control. Her shoulders shook with sobs. She reached in her jeans for the bandanna handkerchief with the Indian on it Sandy had given her on her birthday. Shaking, she buried her face in the bandanna.

What have I done? Harry Atwood asked himself. What do I do now? Kate was on the edge of hysteria. He filled a glass with water and brought it to her. "Drink some water, Kate," he said.

Kate shook her head. She pushed the glass aside and groped her way to the table. She sat down in the single chair and put her head down on arms folded on the table. Finally the sobs diminished. She wiped her eyes with the damp bandanna and sat up. Tomorrow she would think of something; she'd figure a way to get away from Mr. Atwood. He couldn't watch her every minute of the day.

She followed him out of the kitchen into the dark interior of a long hallway with doors on either side. Mr. Atwood turned on a dim light, which illuminated a wide stairway with a heavy, carved banister. It smelled of wax like the bureau in her room after her mother had polished it. Up the steps she went after Mr. Atwood's heavy steps to a wider hallway on the second floor. Mr. Atwood opened a door and stood to one side.

"Up here, Kate," he said. "That will be your room for a while." He switched on another dim light.

This stairway was narrower and had a musty smell. At the top she sensed she was in a large room with a sloping ceiling. Mr. Atwood went past her to turn on a wall lamp. It was a large room. The ceiling pushed down on both sides to small windows with small panes. Lined up neatly against the wall were toys and dollhouses and half-filled bookcases and a tricycle that looked brand new. Under one window was a wooden bunk bed covered with a patchwork quilt. Mr. Atwood went into another room and turned on the light, then switched it off.

"This is the bathroom, Kate. I'm going to leave you now. You'll be warm enough. You can't open the windows. I nailed them shut to keep them from rattling in the winter winds. Have a good night's sleep. Tomorrow's another day. Don't try to leave. I'm going to lock the door to the room and the door at the bottom of the steps. After a while we'll find you a better room on the second floor. Good-night, Kate!"

Kate heard the click of the lock, then the click of another one downstairs. She stood on the bed and looked out the small window. In the dark she could make out the outline of the garage and the trees beyond. In the distance, lightning flashed. Kate began to count. She reached eleven before she heard the first roll of thunder. Her father had taught her the trick of counting after you saw the lightning. The storm was still many miles away. She took off her shoes and jacket and crept under the comforter. When the storm reached the house, driving the heavy rain against her window and illuminating the room with flashes of lightning, Kate was asleep.

Harry Atwood sat in his chair in the bedroom, eyes closed, waiting for the storm to pass. By the time the rain slackened he felt rested. The first thing to do was bring some food into the house. The supermarket in Madison's little shopping center stayed open until ten. He went there from time to time, not often. He would go there tonight. Tomorrow he would drive over to the stores in Manchester to take care of new clothes for Kate. He would buy her something really nice so when she started school someday, she would be the best dressed girl in her class. Kate would like that. In the meantime maybe she would like a cat. The kids out on the town road had put a sign up offering free kittens. He wondered if a cat in the house would make him sneeze.

He put on his plastic raincoat and went down the back steps to the car. The Buick's lights reflected in the fresh puddles in the lane. The trees bent in the strong north winds that followed the storm. Atwood felt in control again, the way he always did when he drove away from the house with its persistent memories. He felt protected as he drove down the roads and highways of New Hampshire from town to town doing his job.

The assistant manager and a teenager at the checkout counter were the only people in the supermarket. The assistant manager nodded at Harry Atwood. "Bad night out, isn't it, sir? Bill and I were talking about closing up early when we saw your lights outside. You're the only customer we've had in the last hour."

Atwood smiled. He came here very seldom and could not remember seeing this man before. Well, he would be coming here more often now, he might as well get acquainted. He took a shopping cart and started down the aisle. He was confused by the great number and variety of foods on the shelf. He had not seriously shopped for a long time, even before Margaret left. What did the three of them used to eat? He could not remember. What was it that Sharon carried to school in her lunch box? He realized he needed help.

"Look," he said to the assistant manager. "My niece has come to stay with me while her mother is in the hospital. She's a ten-year-old girl. I wonder if you could help me get the right things for her to eat. Are you a father?"

"I have three kids, and one of them is a girl, almost twelve now. They all like different things, but they manage to eat us out of house and home. Every time my wife complains about my hours at the store, I tell her I couldn't afford to take another job. I'm only joking, of course, but working here does help, I can tell you."

He led Harry Atwood up and down the aisles. At first he asked if Atwood wanted this and that; then he began to fill the cart without asking.

Looking into the cart, Harry Atwood realized that he had no oven and no freezer. He explained this to the manager who shook his head in disbelief. "You're going to be eating a lot out of the can," he remarked. "What do you cook on, a hot plate?"

Harry Atwood did indeed cook his egg and boil his water on a two-burner hot plate. Margaret had sometimes used the wood stove, but he never bothered. "That's all I have," he answered. "I eat out most of the time. If my niece stays very long, I'll buy a regular stove and a new refrigerator."

The assistant manager now chose more carefully. At last he wheeled the carriage to the counter and told Bill to ring it up.

"Sixty-seven dollars and twenty-three cents, sir," Bill said and began to bag the groceries.

Atwood looked in his wallet. He had only thirty-five dollars. "Will you take a check?" he asked.

"Sure," said Bill. "Over at the cashier's window. Give it to Mr. Timmons along with your driving license."

Mr. Timmons looked at the check and license. He nodded. He copied the license number on the back of the check and initialed it. He handed them back with a smile. "There you are. Thanks a lot for coming in. We are glad to see you again, Mr. Bemis."

13

A little after nine Sunday morning Chief Torbert rang Agatha Bates. "Why don't you come over and have coffee with us? We'll bring you up to date on what we've found out about Kate's disappearance, which isn't much, and we can talk about what to do next."

"Lydia Prescott and Sandy are staying with me," Agatha said. "I'd like to have them come along."

"They're welcome enough, Agatha, but tell them not to get their hopes up."

Malcolm and Vincent Sansone looked tired. Parker McDonald was nodding in a chair, his feet up on the radiator. His head jerked back and forth as he tried to stay awake. They have been up all night, Agatha thought. She felt a twinge of regret for having judged Torbert so harshly yesterday.

The chief offered Lydia and Agatha a cup of strong

black coffee. "One of Vincent's friends left some cider and doughnuts last night, Sandy," he said. "Would that be all right for you? We don't let anyone under twenty-one drink this coffee."

"Have you found out anything about Kate?" Lydia asked anxiously.

Chief Torbert looked at Lieutenant Sansone and shook his head. "Nothing much we didn't already know or guess at. An officer from the state police did come by last night. The tire marks are what you might expect, studded Goodyear tires. They're going to check for fingerprints this morning. How many black cars did your computer tell you were registered in the state, Vincent?"

"About ten thousand, counting limousines and hearses. We can break it down further if we have to, but it doesn't seem practical right now."

"We talked to the folks at the general store. They had nothing to offer beyond what they told Sandy and Agatha. We talked with Mrs. Sinisalo and some other mothers. They kind of agree that a black car with a man inside parked across from the school two afternoons for sure the first week and a half of school. He seems to have left when the other cars left."

"What direction was he headed?" Agatha asked. "Cars park in both directions over there."

Chief Torbert smiled. "I try not to make the same mistake twice. He was headed this way, toward Winthrop Road, as if he came in from Upton. And we have a call in to Janet Petry in North Carolina. Maybe she can place the accent a little closer, now that she's back home. Anything else, Vincent?"

"That about covers it. We're treating it as a kidnapping officially but as a missing child as far as the public is concerned. We won't be able to do that for very long. The guy is a nut, that's for sure, and we don't want to upset him. We've put out an alert in a ten-state area and released the information to the news people. Kate will be on television again."

Agatha Bates nodded her approval. "Have you worked on a profile yet?" she said.

"That's what we wanted to talk about. All the consistencies add up to a big inconsistency. We have to assume Kate did not know the man, but he knew a lot about Kate, enough at least to get her into his car. What did he say to her? If he hadn't pulled down into the Prescotts' road, we could think that he told her Mrs. Prescott had an accident at the Winthrop House, or something like that, and he had come to get her and Sandy."

"He seems to follow certain familiar routines or patterns," Agatha mused. "I think he went to the turnaround because that was a place he knew. It probably made him feel secure in what he had done or was going to do. He'd been watching Kate for three months or more, and it was time to talk to her. I'm not sure he meant to kidnap her. He thought he was doing something perfectly normal. Then Kate did or said something unexpected and he reacted."

"You may be right," Lieutenant Sansone observed.

"Malcolm and I agree that he must have told Kate he knew her mother. From what Sandy says, nothing else would have worked. Tell me, Mrs. Prescott, can you remember a tall, slightly overweight man with glasses, dressed maybe in a business suit, at any of your tables? Someone, perhaps, who let you know that he was familiar with you and your children, or that you were the mother of a famous runaway child?"

"No," Lydia said immediately. "I would remember that. I was always afraid someone was going to engage me in talk about Kate, but no one ever did. There are lots of regulars who eat at the Winthrop House. My sister, Peggy, and I have our favorites but no one such as you describe. I suppose he could have sat somewhere else and watched, just to get something to talk to Kate about. She wouldn't have known. Neither of my girls was ever in the Winthrop House, not until yesterday, that is."

Agatha spoke up. "What kind of people drive regular-sized black cars? I've never seen one in Wingate. Are there any in town, Malcolm?"

"A couple. Businessmen who are on the road a lot. They have to be comfortable and respectable. State cars are usually black, though of course they have state plates. Black is a pretty scarce color in a car these days, I reckon."

"We're working in a thirty-five mile radius, Agatha," Lieutenant Sansone said. "Anything beyond that would not make too much sense. These are some patterns, as you say. We counted the pieces of tinfoil. Then we tested them on Parker here, before he went to sleep. We figure he carries them in his car and put some in his pocket when he came to visit. Depending on whether he ate them continuously or at intervals, we calculate he made twelve to fifteen trips to the trailer and stayed there about an hour."

"Probably when he came this way on business," Chief Torbert added, "he'd stop and see what Kate was up to."

"Then she went back to school," Agatha confirmed, "and he could only watch in the afternoon and Kate wasn't outside, because she had her program. The days were getting shorter. So he decided to get closer. All this must have seemed quite normal, I'm afraid. You must understand, Lydia, that we are now dealing with someone who seems perfectly ordinary and believes that what he is doing is all right. We have no evidence that he is dangerous, but we have to assume he may become dangerous if he is frightened, for example, or threatened."

"What was he doing, Agatha?" Sandy asked. "Why did someone want to talk to Kate? Why didn't he come knocking at the door pretending to be a salesman or something else if he wanted to talk to us? We would have been friendly. It's lonely there when Mom's at work. We live too far away to walk to the lake or the recreation area very often."

"He's someone who couldn't be anyone else other than who he is, Sandy. He's not hiding from anything. But he wanted—deep down, I'm sure, he knew it—more than to talk to Kate. What he really wanted was your sister."

"My God," Lydia Prescott broke out, "what are you saying? What do you mean, he isn't dangerous? He's crazy, that's what he is, stark crazy."

"Not the way you think, Lydia. At least not yet," Chief Torbert assured her. "What Agatha means is that we are dealing with a very complicated person whose normal behavior may not be too different from ours, basically. For some reason he needs Kate, is that it, Agatha?"

"All this is talk," Lydia shouted. "Why does he need my Kate? Why?"

"What we assume, Mrs. Prescott," Lieutenant Sansone spoke quietly, "is that the kidnapper saw Kate on television. She fascinated him, maybe because she reminded him of someone, maybe just because he was drawn to her because she did something dramatic. Stranger things have happened. Maybe he was waiting for Kate to pull another runaway this year. When she didn't, he got curious. For some reason he went into action."

"He's not going to be too hard to locate, Lydia," Agatha Bates said. "We suppose he wants to be found. He probably thinks that will make everything all right and he may even believe he can keep Kate."

"Will he call us?" Lydia wanted to know. "Will he let us know Kate is all right?"

"No, he won't call us, I am pretty sure of that,"
Lieutenant Sansone said. "That would be an admission
he had done something wrong. But we're going to find
him. I'll guarantee you that."

14

The early morning sun slanted through the little window across the room onto Kate's pillow. She turned and threw her arm across her eyes. She was cold and burrowed under the covers. This did not feel like her bed. It was hard, and the springs squeaked. Her fingers touched her clothes. What was she doing in bed in her jeans? The realization of where she was struck her. She jerked herself up and looked around the room. The events of yesterday flooded through her mind: the black car; the smiling Mr. Atwood; the smell of peppermints; the scary, empty kitchen downstairs; and finally, Mr. Atwood's words that this awful place was to be her house.

Shivering, Kate stood up and inspected her surroundings. There was a small bathroom with an old shower stall, a toilet with a wooden seat, and a tiny washbasin. The wallpaper had red and blue puppets on a yellow background. Overhead, a skylight well beyond her reach let in the sunshine. The big room was just a playroom, she guessed, with its two little windows nailed shut, the door to the steps down, and a closet with shelves behind the curtain. Nothing inside there but a couple of camp blankets, some empty boxes, and two rows of books.

The floor was cold under her bare feet. Kate sat on the end of her bed pulling on her socks and shoes and stared, curious, at the toys lined up against the wall. Some kid had a lot of good toys, she thought. They all looked practically new. She wondered if it was the Atwoods' kid. It was a girl, all right. There was a pink plastic doll buggy and four dolls, fancy ones, sitting in chairs around a table set with toy dishes. Kate thought forlornly of her Maggie and Clarissa at the foot of her bed at home waiting for her to come back.

I've got to get out of here, she told herself. She looked out the windows. It was a straight jump down to the ground. No bush or tree underneath either one. Even if she pried a window open, there were no sheets she could tie together. Mr. Atwood had sure put her in a room she couldn't get out of. She had to think of some other way out, maybe some moment she could make a run for it into the woods or the back of the house. Mr. Atwood couldn't watch her all the time.

Kate went to the door and banged hard. She listened to the echo through the house. She heard distant steps, then the lock turning at the bottom of the stairs. Then more steps. Another lock turning. The door opened. Mr.

Atwood stood above her in the doorway, smiling as usual. Today he had on some tan corduroys and a brown plaid woolly shirt.

"Good morning, Kate," he said pleasantly. "I hope you slept all right. There was an awful storm last night. But today is a fine fall day. Perhaps we can take a walk this afternoon and look at the foliage. Come along down. Your breakfast is ready."

Kate followed down the steps, across the dark hallway with its wood-paneled walls, down the other steps to the first floor and back into the kitchen. The first thing she noticed was another chair at the kitchen table, a dining room chair with a plush seat and carving at the back. On the table were three kinds of cereal, a box of sugar doughnuts, and a bowl of apples and pears.

"Do you drink juice, Kate?" Mr. Atwood asked curiously. "I didn't know whether you wanted milk or cocoa. Or maybe your mother lets you drink tea. And I bought a bottle of kid's vitamins."

Kate shook her head. She didn't know what to say. She was hungry, that was for sure. Maybe it was best to be friendly if she planned to make a break for it. There was no point in getting Mr. Atwood mad at her. He was a big man, and there was no telling what he might do if he got excited again.

"Orange juice and cocoa, please, I guess," she said. "Mom makes it for us on Sunday before she goes to work." She sat down and pointed to two of the boxes. "We're not supposed to eat sugar cereal. I'll just have cornflakes."

"An egg?" Mr. Atwood asked.

"No, thank you. I don't like eggs much."

She ate the cornflakes and chewed on a doughnut. Mr. Atwood opened a packet of cocoa mix and poured in hot water. He went to the cupboard and took out a bag of marshmallows. He put one on top of the cocoa, the way Mrs. Reed did at the lunch counter in the general store. Then Mr. Atwood put an egg in the pan of boiling water. He looked at his watch. He tapped his fingers on the counter while he waited. He took the egg out with a spoon and poured the hot water into a cup. He put a tea bag into the cup.

Kate watched him break the egg into a flowered bowl. The egg came out all yellow and runny. Mr. Atwood crumbled half a piece of bread into the bowl and mixed it together with egg.

He ate slowly, never losing his smile whenever he caught Kate's eye across the table. Kate bowed her head and took another doughnut. I don't care what he thinks, she thought. I'm going to dunk my doughnut into my cocoa, the way Sandy and I dunk doughnuts into our milk when Mom isn't watching.

"I bought us a lot of food last night at the supermarket," Mr. Atwood observed. "I'm going to the big mall in Manchester this morning to buy you some clothes. Do you want to help me make a list? Later on, you can go with me, when we are better friends."

Kate did not know what to say. She usually wore Sandy's clothes when they got too small for her sister, plus whatever new things her mother and Aunt Peggy bought her for Christmas and her birthday. "What I have is all right," she said softly. "Sandy and I don't pay much attention to what we wear."

"I've noticed that, Kate. But if you are going to start a new life here, you will have to change some of your old habits."

Kate shook her head defiantly. "I don't think so, Mr. Atwood. I get along pretty well the way I am now. My mother says there's no sense in trying to be something you're not."

Mr. Atwood lost his smile. "Your mother isn't here now. I'm the one who's here and I have the responsibility to look after you. Try to understand that, Kate. Looking after someone is an important responsibility. Well, I'll just have to do what I can myself. And I'm going to buy an electric stove and a new refrigerator for us, too," he said proudly. He remembered the kittens down the road. "And a kitten," he announced. "We'll get ourselves a kitten. Won't that be nice? You'd like that, wouldn't you, Kate? Little girls like kittens."

Kate hated kittens. They made her sneeze and were always running off when you wanted to hold them. A dog, maybe, yes. She and Sandy had talked about a dog lots of times, but Mom kept avoiding the subject. She shook her head again. "I don't think so. I don't like cats very much, Mr. Atwood. They make me sneeze."

Mr. Atwood pursed his lips. He tapped his fingers on the table. Kate was going to be difficult, he realized.

Well, she would have to learn. He took off his glasses and rubbed his eyes. Without his glasses, Kate noticed, he didn't look so friendly. She didn't like the way he stared at her, squinting a little bit with his pale-blue eyes. He muttered something Kate could not make out and put his glasses back on.

The smile returned. "Maybe if we're starting out together," he said slowly, "you should know something. My name isn't really Harry Atwood. It's Harry Bemis. That's what you better call me from now on. Mr. Bemis or Harry, if you like."

The admission was too much for Kate to comprehend. "But you said your name was Harry Atwood, and," she paused, "you let me call you Mr. Atwood. What's going on? Who are you, anyway?"

"I'm not sure now," the man answered. "Harry Bemis, I suppose. Bemis was my father's name, but I never liked it. My mother was an Atwood, Rose Atwood. That's a very fine family name down in Atlanta, where I come from. I guess I always wanted to be an Atwood, and I must have decided yesterday afternoon I was going to change my name if I was going to change everything else."

There was something really wrong with Mr. Atwood—or Mr. Bemis, if that was his name—Kate realized. She felt less secure with someone whose real name was Harry Bemis. What could she say? Suddenly, Mr. Bemis, the man without his glasses and the pale-blue eyes, was a stranger to her.

He seemed to understand what she was thinking. "Look, it's all right if you keep on calling me Mr. Atwood if you want to. That's how we met, isn't it? If we go out together, to town or somewhere, you could call me Mr. Bemis or, better still, Harry. Maybe after a while, you will call me Dad." He stopped for a moment. He bit his bottom lip nervously. "And I wonder, Kate, I wonder if I could call you Sharon? Would you mind?"

"Sharon!" Kate shrieked. The name struck the deepest nerve of dislike. "Sharon! Sharon Emerson is the worst kid in school. She's a full-time wimp. She's a tattletale and a liar and the nastiest girl I've ever known. Nobody likes Sharon. I'd rather be dead than be called Sharon. My name is Kate, Kate Prescott. That's what I'm going to stay and don't you forget it, Mr. Bemis or Mr. Atwood, or whoever you are."

A dark cloud passed over Mr. Bemis's face. He looked hard and stern. He clenched his hands into fists. "I think you better go to your room. Get up there fast before I lose my temper. I brought your schoolbooks in from the car. They are on the counter. Take them with you, or I may throw them away. Go! I'll lock the doors behind you."

15

Chief Torbert and Lieutenant Sansone walked to the front steps with Lydia Prescott, Sandy, and Agatha Bates. They were greeted by a woman and a man with a television camera.

"Pat Burke from Channel Nine News, Chief Torbert. I've come back to see you," the woman shouted. "Can you tell us anything about Kate Prescott? Do you think she's run away? It's about time she took off again, isn't it? Some people in town say she was kidnapped. What can you tell us?"

Vincent Sansone whispered in Torbert's ear.

"We're working on both possibilities," Malcolm Torbert answered slowly. "Kate seems to have taken a ride Friday afternoon with a man we have not yet identified. Whether she went on her own account we do not know. We have no evidence she was carried off violently. As you see, the state police are assisting us. This is Lieutenant Vincent Sansone. Lieutenant Agatha Bates, formerly of the Boston Police Department, is also giving us a hand. That's about all I can tell you."

Pat Burke looked disappointed. She turned to Sansone. "What do you know about the man, Lieutenant? It doesn't sound to me as though you've told us everything."

"I can't tell you any more than Chief Torbert has. We hope to have enough to identify the individual fairly soon."

"What do you mean by that?" the reporter insisted.

Lieutenant Sansone shook his head. "Just what I said, Pat." He and Malcolm Torbert went back into the building.

Lydia Prescott was weeping. She bent her head down to hide the tears. Sandy put her arm around her mother's waist. The man with the camera moved in closer. Agatha Bates stepped in front of the camera. "Will you stop that now, please?"

"You have enough, Eddie," Pat Burke said. Then, in a gentle voice she asked Lydia, "Are you worried, Mrs. Prescott? Your daughter showed up the last two times she disappeared. Don't you think she'll show up this time?"

Head still down, Lydia walked away without answering. Agatha paused to say a few words to the reporter. "I know you have your job to do and we don't always tell you everything you want to know, but please leave Mrs. Prescott alone. There's nothing at all she can tell you."

"What about you, Lieutenant Bates? What can you tell us? What are you doing on the case?"

"Very little. I live in Wingate now. I'm just a friend of Chief Torbert and Sandy Prescott."

"Do you really think you're going to find the person who drove off with Kate?" Pat Burke demanded.

Agatha thought for a minute. She was certain the stranger would be watching the evening news. They should begin to deal with him now. "Yes," she replied confidently. "I think we will, and fairly soon." She followed Lydia and Sandy across the street.

In Agatha's living room, Lydia looked helpless. She was fighting to bring herself under control. Tom had jumped into her lap. Lydia scratched the purring cat behind his ears. "I only wish now I had bought the girls a dog. They've always wanted one. A dog might have come down the road to meet Kate and she wouldn't have taken the ride."

"Don't torment yourself, Lydia. You've done what you had to do for your family," Agatha assured her. "You must believe that Kate didn't let you down again. She got into the car because she had some reason for trusting the man. He must have convinced her it would be all right with you. He went down your lane with her and they talked. These are not the usual actions of someone who takes a child. We can only guess what happened after that."

"Is she in danger, Agatha? The man must be insane."

Agatha considered the question. There was no point in

lying to Lydia Prescott. She had already begun to fear the
worst. Something had gone wrong at the end of the lane.
Someone had carried Kate off. Someone had not brought
her back or turned her loose. What had happened down
by the deserted trailers? Someone, she guessed, had
become rattled and made the mistake of driving away
with Kate. Now he could not deal with the consequences.
That had to mean he was a respected member of a
community. Now he must be justifying his act and trying
to convince Kate it was all right. She was probably in no
danger now, but when they came to take him, what then?

"Right now, I think Kate is safe enough, Lydia,
wherever she is, which is probably not very far from
here. The man's car, his dress, his manner, his routine,
the way he waited at the school—these are helpful signs.
We have to rely on what he is or was. But I'm afraid,
frankly, he will not want to give himself up when we find
him. And he won't want to give Kate up. The way he
looks at it, they are in this together. He has made her into
a kind of partner. He needs her. There may be problems
later on."

Sandy had listened silently to the talk in the police
station and in the living room. Why was everyone sitting
around talking and waiting? Why weren't they out
looking for her sister? "How do you know so much about
this guy?" she asked Agatha almost rudely. "Why isn't
everyone out looking for him? Why aren't the police
checking all the summer places?"

Agatha ignored Sandy's anger. "The police are doing

their job. They're checking the private and state mental hospitals. They have circulated what they know to all the local law enforcement people. I'm sure they have started in on the summer homes. I don't think we are looking for a summer resident. He has taken Kate, almost certainly, to where he lives. It can't be too far away. He must live by himself. Just a little more information and every law officer in five states will have a good profile of the man we're after. And that will do the trick. Just be patient, Sandy. All we can do is wait for someone to turn him up for us. Something is going to happen soon."

"Did you ever have a case like this?" Sandy asked.

Agatha turned her memory back through thirty years of police work. A long time ago, she recalled, she had helped Lieutenant Finnegan on an adoption case. "Not quite," she said, "but sort of. A family had adopted a baby girl. When she was ten or eleven, the adoptive mother died. The real mother came back with a claim for her child. The court sided with her and told the adoptive father to give the child up. He disappeared for several months, I remember. When we located him, he barricaded himself in an apartment with the girl."

Lydia had been listening to the story. "What happened, Agatha?"

"Nothing very good," she answered. "I'm going to fix lunch now." She went into the kitchen, closing the door behind her. Why had she remembered that case? It wasn't at all the same, of course, but the details of what happened then and what was happening now insisted on crowding together in her mind.

The man who took Kate off had followed a pattern. Agatha imagined him sitting alone in his house watching television and seeing Kate for the first time. Then again last year she showed up on the set. Kate must have reminded him of a daughter who had died or been taken off by a divorced mother. This year he waited for Kate to run away again. When she didn't, he convinced himself he ought to find out about her. He started to track her down. That had to be how it happened. She would talk it over after lunch with Torbert and Sansone. In the meantime it looked like tomato soup and toasted cheese sandwiches for lunch.

At three the phone rang. Agatha grabbed it before it could ring again and awaken Sandy and her mother, whom she had persuaded to try to rest. It was Malcolm Torbert. "I think we're onto something, Agatha. Could you come over? I'd leave the Prescotts there if I were you."

Malcolm and Vincent Sansone were still drinking coffee and listening to the radio. Parker MacDonald had disappeared. The school principal, they explained, had asked to organize teams of parents and kids to search the woods and check out the summer places. They wanted to help and Torbert had agreed. Half an hour ago, a sixteen-year-old boy, Ken Steckler, showed up with his father. They were on one of the teams and Ken heard about the black car and the man waiting at the school. He remembered that last June he was hitching over to Winthrop. A black car—a Buick, he was certain—

stopped to pick him up. The driver went down Old Winthrop Road instead of Route 219. The man started to talk about Kate Prescott and how she must be the town celebrity. Ken pointed out where they lived as they drove past. The driver swung down the lane and turned around. He asked about the trailers. Then he took Ken over to Winthrop. When he told his father today, Mr. Steckler brought his son into the station.

"Our stranger, was it?" Agatha observed.

"Yes," said Lieutenant Sansone. "Big guy, dark suit, rimless glasses, friendly but sort of quiet."

"You didn't get me over here to tell me that," Agatha said.

"You're right," Malcolm answered. "Young Ken is a bumper-sticker freak. He collects them and puts them on big boards. His father said the playroom walls are covered with them. Anyway, he watched the Buick drive off. It had a bumper sticker he'd never seen before on the rear bumper—'Insurance is the Best Policy.'"

"We have enough now, Agatha, don't you think?" Sansone asked. "Friendly man, black car, business dress, nice and friendly. A definite insurance type, I'd say."

"I think you can add something else," Agatha Bates said. She told them she was convinced the man was a father replacing a daughter. Someone would know him. People in most small towns knew about divorces and deaths.

"Yes," Sansone agreed. "That should clinch it. I'll have headquarters get a revised description out. We'll let it out for the late evening news."

"Yes," said Agatha, "everything but the bit about the daughter. That might be too much. Let's not surprise him. Give him time to think about it. He might decide to give Kate up."

"If he doesn't?" Malcolm Torbert asked.

"Then *we* will have to think about it, Malcolm," Agatha replied.

16

Kate sat on the edge of the bunk bed and listened to the angry stomp of Mr. Atwood, or Mr. Bemis, whatever his name was, down the stairs and into, she supposed, the kitchen. Then a door slammed and moments later she heard a car start up. In a few seconds the sound faded. The house was silent.

She remembered that it was Saturday, which was a pretty good day at home. Mom let them sleep while she prepared something special for their breakfast, doughnuts, pancakes, or French toast. Half an hour before she left for work, she rang the get-out-of-bed bell. She put the money on the counter along with the weekly shopping list. Unless the weather was really bad, Kate and Sandy would take their canvas tote bags and walk in to Wingate. They would spend an hour in the general store, looking at the prices and trying to make the best selections. Mom always included a dollar for each of them to spend. They usually saved one dollar for Mom's birthday present and divided up the other one for bubble gum or penny, really nickel, candy. After that they went to the gym or library for another hour. It wasn't much, but they were free to do what they wanted, and that was what mattered.

She looked at her schoolbooks on the floor beside the bed. The class had started to study about the Pilgrims, who didn't interest Kate very much. She dropped the books back onto the floor. Mr. Whatever-his-name-was had said she wouldn't need them for a while. She went to the window facing the back of the house. She measured the space with her eyes. She could probably squeeze through if she had to, like maybe if the house caught on fire and she was trapped. The thought frightened her. She tried to move the nails holding the bottom half of the window shut. They were in tight. She would need a hammer or pliers to get them loose.

There was a toy box against the wall. She rummaged among the plastic figures and blocks. There was nothing heavy enough to use. There was nothing in the bathroom. She pushed the hanging cloth aside to look in the closet. The books were no good. Neither were the bent wire coat hangers on a narrow cross pipe. Kate studied the pipe. It rested on two metal braces. She lifted it up. It was something she could try, at least. She fitted the pipe over the nail and worked it back and forth. The nail was deep into the wood, but gradually she worked it loose. She wrapped her Indian head bandanna around her fingers and twisted and pulled. At last the nail slipped out.

She repeated the process on the other side. It took longer there, but eventually the two nails lay on the sill. Kate struggled to push the window up. She stuck her head out; the space *was* big enough to slip through. Maybe if there was a fire, someone would be underneath to catch her. Or maybe she could ask for sheets. She closed the window and pushed the nails back into place.

What was she going to do the rest of the day? Mr. Atwood—Kate decided to stick with the name she first knew him by—wouldn't be back until the afternoon, she was sure. Shopping in a mall took a lot of time. Kate went into the closet to look over the books. They were little kids' books, Mother Goose and picture books and animal alphabets. At the end of the shelf was an album, a fancy leather one like the kind she and Sandy wanted to get for Mom when they had enough money.

She took it into her room. She shoved a goopy-looking doll off one of the little wooden chairs, pushed the china set to one side, and sat down to open the album. There were lots of photographs and some kid's artwork and at the back, a lot of clippings.

Kate decided to start at the beginning. On the first page was a picture of a little baby taken in what looked like a hospital. The baby didn't look like much. Someone had written underneath, "Sharon, two days old." Kate's throat tightened. She felt her heart thump faster. She turned the page. There standing in front of the door of a brick home were a woman holding the baby and Mr. Atwood. They were pretty happy.

Kate looked closely at the woman. It must be Margaret, who didn't live here anymore. It was hard to tell, but in back of her smile she looked worried about something, maybe the baby. Underneath the picture, the writing told Kate the kid was Sharon with her mother and father. More pictures of Sharon followed, sometimes with her mother or a friend: birthday parties, swimming in a pool, playing with other kids. There weren't many pictures of Mr. Atwood. Maybe he was taking the pictures. Mrs. Atwood always looked worried.

What a big house, Kate thought enviously, with a swimming pool and a super swing set and playhouse. And lots of yard to run around in. Every once in a while the word Atlanta appeared. That must be where they lived. She knew there was a football team from Atlanta that showed up every once in a while on the Sunday television. Kate reckoned it was somewhere down South.

It was sort of fun watching the kid grow up, even if her name was Sharon. Margaret kept her in fancy clothes. Her hair was always brushed with a ribbon or barrette at the back. Looking at Sharon when she was about four, Kate sensed an uncomfortable recognition taking shape in her head. She felt that she was looking at herself, or at least some pictures of herself in Mom's notebook album. Now she turned the pages only to study the resemblance. When she reached five, Sharon was a ringer for Kate Prescott. It was really weird.

On her sixth birthday Sharon and her mother stood in
the snow just in front of a big porch of a large stone
house. Sharon was in ski pants and a jacket with a fur
collar. Kate looked carefully at the house. Up at the top,
the third floor under the roof, was a small window. It was
her window. The Atwoods had moved to this place.
Someone had written "February, in Madison" under the
picture. There weren't many photographs after that and
they were mostly close-ups of Sharon. The last one was
of Sharon in a plaid skirt and woolly sweater and knee
stockings and lace-up shoes. She held up a Mickey
Mouse lunch box. She stood stiff and uncertain in a
driveway. She looked worried, like her mother. The label
said, "Madison, Sharon's first school day." Kate
thumbed through the artwork. It was like the stuff her
mother saved from what she and Sandy had drawn years
ago: smiling faces with stick arms, dumb-looking birds
with kids' faces, dogs with five legs—maybe one of
them was a tail—and buildings that looked as though
they were falling down.

The rest of the album was filled with newspaper-
clipping stories and pictures. The first was a large picture
of Sharon, which Kate had seen a page or two back. Big
printed letters under the picture read, "Madison First-
Grader Missing."

Kate read the news story under the picture. On
September 19—Kate counted back five years—Sharon
Bemis had got off the school bus at the end of her lane.
Mrs. Bemis had just begun to walk from the house to the

town road to meet Sharon. She told police she heard the bus stop and then go on. A minute or so later she heard a car door slam. Sharon did not come down the lane. There was no sign of her at the town road. Mrs. Bemis assumed that her husband had come early and taken Sharon into Madison on an errand. When Harry Bemis came home alone at four-thirty, they notified the police of Sharon's absence.

Kate skimmed the clippings trying to find the one that brought Sharon Bemis home. She did not find one. There were, it seemed, hundreds of clippings before they began to thin out to one or two occasional stories about the still-missing first-grader. All anyone really knew was that a car had apparently followed the school bus out of sight. Sharon had begun to walk toward her house. The car stopped at the edge of the lane, a man's footsteps followed her. There were signs of a scuffle and the man's footsteps returned to the car. Nothing else. No further trace of Sharon Bemis was ever found.

Kate went back through the clippings. Harry Bemis and his family had moved to Madison from Atlanta in February. Mr. Bemis was district head of Allied Insurance of North America. He spent most of his time on the road. He admitted that his wife had not been happy about the move to Madison. The pictures of Harry Bemis were of a younger man, with a lot of hair and no glasses. He looked like a pretty good dad to Kate. There were no interviews with Margaret. It was reported that she collapsed the day after Sharon's disappearance and was in the care of physicians.

The last clipping was from three years ago on the second anniversary of Sharon's disappearance. A reporter reviewed the case, talking to state and local police and people in Madison. The police were still following up on unlikely or remote leads. Margaret Bemis had returned to her family in Atlanta after a lengthy stay in a hospital. It was assumed she blamed her husband for bringing his family to a lonely house in the New Hampshire countryside. Apparently there was a divorce. Mr. Bemis refused to talk about Sharon's disappearance or his wife. He appeared in Madison from time to time. He was still friendly, but no one really knew what to say to him.

The last page in her album was a fuzzy picture of Sharon on a torn missing children's report. She looked worried.

Kate closed the album and tucked it back into place on the shelf. She felt as though she had uncovered a horrible family secret. She felt guilty with this knowledge about Mr. Atwood. She understood a lot of things now, but she was not reassured. She told herself she had better keep her mouth shut about what she had learned. She had enough trouble with Mr. Atwood as it was. There was no telling what he might do. She lay back on her bed. Tomorrow maybe, if I'm good, I'll get downstairs or outside and make a break for it. That hope in mind, she fell asleep.

17

The trip to the mall had been difficult. The women in the stores kept asking Harry Bemis questions that he couldn't answer, like shoe sizes, color preferences, whether he wanted school clothes, play clothes, party clothes. He was embarrassed. This was not what he expected. Now he felt unsure about the boxes of clothes that filled the trunk of the Buick. What if Kate didn't like them? That didn't matter, he told himself. Anything was better than the rags she was wearing now.

It would be better to wait until tomorrow to give her the clothes. Today was a day for discipline. Kate had to be taught she couldn't scream at him if they were going to be friends. That was the trouble with Margaret. She never rebuked Sharon, who had her own way in everything. When he spoke sharply to the child, Margaret gave him a disapproving look and put her arm around Sharon to protect her. Kids needed discipline these days. Look at the way they talked and dressed and acted. Kate wouldn't grow up like that, he would see to it.

Maybe he would give her the small television he bought for her room. After letting the salesman sell him a gigantic refrigerator and an electric stove with a control panel like an airplane's, Harry Bemis had caught sight of a television that would be just right for Kate: a small color set that had a stereo radio and a cassette player. He pondered the choice of colors, finally settling on pink. That was a girl's color.

He relaxed in the familiar seat of the Buick. He and Kate would start over tomorrow. He would forget about the kitten. And if she wanted to be Kate, that would be all right, too. He didn't want her to grow up like Sharon. What made him think that he should call her Sharon? He was wrong. That part of his life was past. He wondered if he should change his name to Atwood, the way he had always wanted to. Harry Atwood sounded a lot better than Harry Bemis. He would have to think it over.

He passed the sub and pizza shop a couple of miles outside of Madison, colored light bulbs framing the front of the building. He pulled over to the side of the road and backed up. Kate could have a sandwich for supper. He ordered her a large sub with everything on it along with a pint carton of chocolate milk and a bag of potato chips. For himself, ham on a bulky roll. In the car he switched on his lights. It was getting dark early these days.

Kate half heard the kitchen door slammed shut followed by the sound of steps in the kitchen. She wiped the sleep from her eyes and turned in the dim light. It was almost dark outside. She was hungry and lonely and more scared than she had ever been before, even that evening when she and Sandy listened to her mother tell Dad she and the girls were leaving and her father had acted like a crazy man. Kate sat on the edge of her bed; she squeezed her arms tight around her chest and rocked back and forth.

Mr. Atwood unlocked the door. He was holding something in his left hand behind his back. Kate smelled the sub. Maybe it was going to be all right. She watched Mr. Atwood put the sub and a carton of milk and some chips on the doll table. He put something down in the shadows by the door while he unscrewed the dim bulb and replaced it with a bulb that lit up the whole room.

"I brought you a present, Kate. Mind you, I'm still upset with your behavior, and you will have to stay in your room until tomorrow, when we'll start over. We'll try to be friends again. Anyway, it's Saturday night. There must be some good programs on. What do you think?" He handed her the television set.

Kate held it in her lap. It was really something. "Thank you, Mr. Atwood," she made herself say. "It must have been really expensive."

"It was, Kate, but I have no one else to spend my money on. Anyway, you'll need it during the day when I go off to work. You won't miss your programs anymore. There's your supper. As I said, we'll try to start over tomorrow. If it's a good day, we'll take a walk."

Kate watched him leave, then began to search the baseboard for an outlet. She found it in back of the dolls. She plugged the set in and turned it on. It was color! Kate unwrapped the delicious-smelling sub. Chewing happily, she switched the channels. Mr. Atwood, the prison room, the album in the closet, her fears and loneliness faded away as she found a familiar program and settled back for an evening of television.

Harry Bemis sat in his study on the first floor also looking at television. He was just in time for the six o'clock news on channel nine. It was the usual succession of disasters, but nothing about a missing child from Wingate, New Hampshire. He was right, he congratulated himself. No one was going to pay attention to Kate's disappearance this time, at least not for a while. By then he would have made some plans.

He picked up the album from the corner of the desk. He turned the plastic pages. He noted there was room for some more clippings. Maybe by the middle of next week, he could fill in the empty pages. Thumbing back through the album he realized once more how much Kate looked like Sharon. She certainly didn't act like Sharon. Kate was tough. He supposed it was good she had spirit. She could look after herself. Like me, he thought; he had always looked after himself.

He hadn't been able to look after Margaret and Sharon, he thought bitterly. Early on, they had formed a team and closed the door against him. After a while it seemed that he spent more time alone in his Buick than he did in his home with his family.

He recalled the shock on Margaret's face when she saw the house in Madison he had bought for them. She stood in the snow at the back door, looking at the place in disbelief. "It's a wreck, Harry. It's a desolate wreck at the end of nowhere." Her disbelief turned to sorrow and silence when she saw the inside. Holding Sharon close to her, she made her way from room to room, shaking her head.

"You told me to find a place for us, Margaret," he had protested. "You weren't interested in helping. You didn't even want to come when I got the promotion to the New Hampshire district. Look," his tone softened, "we're going to fix it up, Margaret. We can sort of start over again up here. It won't be like in Atlanta. It's a grand house for this part of the world. That can be your job, furnishing and decorating our new home."

But Margaret had, without saying so, refused. She sulked. She prepared meals out of a can on the hot plate. They used—or didn't use—the old summer furniture. She ignored his suggestions to call in electricians and plumbers and carpenters. She kept the kitchen spotless. She and Sharon sat there at the table in front of an electric heater, playing games and piecing together puzzles.

"It's your house, Harry," she said. "Do whatever you want to. It's not ours."

He had done nothing. Winter turned to a muddy spring

and spring turned to a damp, chill summer, the worst in twenty years, the local people said. Once a week Margaret and Sharon went to the supermarket and town library. They returned with cans of food and piles of books. Margaret sat at the kitchen table reading to Sharon. The child had acquired her mother's worried look. She lowered her eyes when Harry came into the kitchen. She answered his questions in quiet, respectful tones.

Before school started, Margaret ordered Sharon's wardrobe from fancy children's catalogues. Even the lunch box came from California, not the mall in Madison.

Then, one sunny afternoon in September, about this time of year, it was finished. Sharon was gone. Six months later Margaret was gone. Only Harry Bemis remained in the stone summer house, which sank into deeper dilapidation.

Harry roused himself from his morbid thoughts. He had work to do, the reports that he prepared every weekend. But things would change now. He would get the carpenter in, and the plumber, and the electrician. The old house would have its face lifted. One day Kate would be proud of where she lived.

18

"The stove and refrigerator will be here on Wednesday," Harry Bemis told Kate at the kitchen table. "We're going to fix up some other things, too, like the back steps and the veranda out front. I'll get Mr. Higgins in to cut the brush back and keep the field mowed. It will be a nice place for your friends to come and visit."

Kate wasn't listening to Mr. Atwood's plans. She ate her doughnut and waited. He had said they would take a walk. He didn't look like much of a runner. She figured if she got a good start into the woods, she had a chance to make it. She snapped to attention; Mr. Atwood was asking about the television set.

"Oh, it's good, Mr. Atwood. Thanks again. I stayed up until eleven. Mom never lets me stay up that late, even on Saturday nights. Sandy can if she wants to, but ten o'clock is my limit."

Harry Bemis smiled indulgently. "If you're a good girl, Kate, you may stay up until eleven on Friday and Saturday nights when you want to. After a while, I hope we can look at it together in my study."

He watched Kate take another doughnut and dip it in her chocolate milk. She was a good kid. He felt a growing affection for her. With Sharon it had been different. Margaret was between Sharon and him. The way he felt now at the kitchen table with Kate this morning, this was probably the way fathers were supposed to feel.

"Maybe I was a little hard on you yesterday, Kate," he half apologized. "But it was for your own good. I believe in discipline, just as my mother did. Kids have to learn where they stand. Anyway, I've been thinking about it. You don't have to be a Sharon here. It was just an idea I had. Sharon seemed like a nice name for a girl. I was probably wrong. We'll let you keep on being Kate. Are you still hungry? I have another box of doughnuts."

Kate shook her head. She was tense with anticipation. When were they going outside? She dared not ask. Mr. Atwood liked to decide what would happen.

"Well, then, it's back to your room for a while. If the sun stays out, I'll think about taking you for a walk across the field. I have a lot of work to do this morning. Sunday is the day I write my reports."

Upstairs, Kate felt like a caged animal. There was nothing worth watching Sunday mornings, just cartoons she had seen a hundred times before and lots of preachers. She started to read some poems from Mother Goose, but the pictures were sort of dumb and she put the book down.

Cautiously she removed the nails and opened the window. She looked at the woods. They stretched around toward the front of the house. They looked pretty thick. She stared down at the ground. It wasn't any closer. Two sheets wouldn't get her very far. She did some knee bends, the way they did in gym, to loosen her muscles, then some deep-breathing exercises. She had to be ready.

At noon Mr. Atwood fetched her down to the kitchen. He had prepared a plate of apples, crackers, and cheese. Boxes were piled behind her chair. Mr. Atwood instructed her to open them. His smile was a little anxious and uncertain, Kate thought. One by one, she opened the boxes, realizing with each one that the clothes inside were meant for a Sharon.

When they lay opened all around her chair, she said, "They're awfully nice and I guess I should be grateful; but, you see, I don't wear these kinds of clothes. They're kind of formal. Kids at school would tease me about them. Anyway," she added, "where am I going to wear them, up in my cell?" She realized as soon as the words came out, she had said the wrong thing.

Harry Bemis bit his lip. Kate was right, but she couldn't be allowed to say rude things that hurt other people's feelings. "When you can be trusted to get out of your cell, Kate, you may want to put something decent on so I can be proud of you. Until then, please fold them up and put them back in the boxes. I'll store them in the living room. You may tell me when you want them. You better take the underwear and shirt and jeans upstairs. You need a change of clothes. Bring your jacket down."

Kate folded the new clothes as well as she could. Then she raced upstairs, the first time by herself. She didn't stop to poke around on the second floor. She threw the underwear and jeans on the bed, seized her jacket, and raced down the steps. "I'm ready," she announced. "I can use some fresh air."

"Good," Mr. Atwood said. "I'm not going to put you on a leash. Please stay close. I mean it. You have played enough games with me."

Out the back door and around the corner of the house they walked along side by side. Harry Bemis felt warm and protecting toward Kate as they made their first expedition together.

"Where does the lane go?" Kate asked innocently.

"Down to Town Forest Road, which goes into town." Mr. Atwood began to point out how different trees had different-colored leaves, which fell at different times. First the swamp maples and the sumacs, then the ash and the hickory. After that the glorious sugar maples. Some of the red oaks held on to their dry brown leaves almost until spring.

They walked across the overgrown meadow toward the tree line. Kate measured the distance. Come on, she said to herself. Come on, Mr. Atwood, keep on going. Aloud she asked, "Do you have all those kinds of trees here?"

A fallen-down rock wall marked the edge of the field. Mr. Atwood bent down to pick up a brilliant red-and-yellow leaf. "This is a sugar maple. We don't have too many of these any more. People tell me they seem to be dying out." He handed it to Kate. "Here, take it up to your room."

They were at a break in the wall. It's now or never, Kate thought. "Where are the hickory trees?" she asked. Mr. Atwood looked up into the branches. "They are all mixed in. Most of their leaves have fallen. There's one there." He walked toward the wall to retrieve a yellow leaf.

Kate bolted. Through the gap and between the trunks, stumbling over dead branches, she headed deeper into the woods. She heard Mr. Atwood shouting after her to stop. She ran faster. There had to be something ahead of her. A road or a house or just someone walking in the woods. All she had to do was stay ahead of Mr. Atwood.

Furious at having been fooled, Harry Bemis charged after Kate. His glasses fell to the ground. Breathing hard, he stooped to retrieve them. He was not in condition for a chase. He had better catch Kate quickly. She was out of sight now, but he could hear scuffling steps ahead of him. She was headed into the deepest part of the town forest. "You've made a bad mistake, Kate Prescott," he said half aloud. "It's over a mile to the other side."

Kate fled on. Her legs began to ache. Her chest burned, sweat trickled down into her eyes. Mr. Atwood was still behind her, maybe closer. She heard his heavy breathing. Rubbing the sweat from her eyes, she did not see the branch in her path. It poked between her legs and she fell. Helpless, she closed her eyes and waited.

Harry Bemis picked her up roughly. He carried her, unprotesting, under his right arm. It occurred to him that he was stronger than he would have guessed. Over the wall and back across the meadow he strode. Up the steps to the attic playroom. He dropped Kate on her bed.

"I warned you, Kate. You will have to learn the hard way. No supper tonight. I'll put some breakfast inside your door early tomorrow morning, before I leave. We'll talk again tomorrow night when I come home."

He started to leave, then turned to the window and pushed it. One of the nails fell out. "Good for you, Kate!" He laughed. "You have spirit. I like that. I don't recommend you go out the window. It's thirty feet down. I'll leave it open. You may need fresh air after your run."

I almost lost her, he thought, going down the steps. The thought of losing Kate now created panic. Kate was something else. He supposed he had known it for a while, but now he knew it for sure. He couldn't lose her, not ever.

19

Lieutenant Sansone sat alone in the Wingate police station, leaning back in Malcolm Torbert's chair. His head dropped down to his chest. He jerked it back and rubbed his eyes. He took a mouthful of the cold, thick coffee. The clock on the wall told him it was almost nine. Malcolm would be back soon. He had gone home for a short nap and supper. He promised to bring back a sandwich and a thermos of hot coffee. Sansone figured he could stretch out in the cruiser and sleep for an hour or two. He let his head drop forward.

The sound of Torbert's heavy steps in the office and the ringing of the phone at the same time brought him to wakeful attention. He pulled his feet off the desk and took the phone. A slow, deep voice came over the wire. It said it belonged to Charles Postma, chief of police in Madison.

"This is Vincent Sansone," the lieutenant said. "We worked together on the missing child in Madison a while back."

"It's good to talk to you again, Lieutenant Sansone," the voice continued. "We may have something here on Kate Prescott. The description of the man came in late this afternoon. It kicked around for a couple of hours, I'm afraid. Then one of our auxiliaries read it when she came into the office. She called me right away. I think we may have your man living here in town. The description fits all right. Big Buick, big middle-aged guy, businessman, district head of Allied Insurance." Chief Postma paused. "But it doesn't make much sense."

Sansone had begun to write on a pad. He nodded encouragement to Torbert's questioning look. "What do you mean?" he asked.

"The man is Harry Bemis. It was his daughter, Sharon, who disappeared. I can't figure he'd be stealing a kid."

"Harry Bemis. Sharon and Margaret. I blew it," Sansone muttered. "I listened to Agatha Bates and it went in one ear and out the other. I'm sorry," he told Postma. "I was talking to myself. Yes, I remember the family. Big old house a couple of miles out of town. The wife went away when she left the hospital. Bemis stayed on, but he wouldn't talk to us. I agree, it's hard to believe. Do you ever see him in town?"

"He drives through all the time. He goes to the post office regularly. He has an office in Manchester, but he's on the road a lot. He's standoffish. Not unfriendly, mind you, just sort of hard to talk to for more than two or three minutes. He has the sticker on the bumper of the Buick. It might have been him. I've seen stranger things."

"You can't see the house from the road, can you?" Sansone asked. "As I remember, everything was grown up along the lane and around the house. There will be two cruisers there in twenty minutes. Can you tuck them out of sight? Check to see if there are lights on in the house. Is there any kind of road in back of the house?"

"Nothing," Chief Postma replied. "It's all woods, part of town forest land. I'll send two men through the woods to watch the back door. If a car comes out before your cruisers get here, what shall I do?"

Sansone considered the possibilities. There were not many. "Keep your car out of sight. If someone goes in, let the car pass. If someone comes out, block it off and move fast. Chief Torbert and I will be there within an hour. Good work, Charlie."

"I think we've got him, Malcolm, if he's home," Sansone said with a tired smile. He stood up and stretched while he told Torbert the details.

"Harry Bemis, eh," Malcolm said. "I remember the case. Never a trace of the girl, was there?"

"Nothing. She disappeared into thin air."

"Her father must have flipped. We better get Agatha here. It looks like she's our expert on how to deal with Harry. I'll give her a call."

* * *

Harry Bemis waited impatiently for the six o'clock news. By now they must be looking for Kate. He watched a succession of fires, European trade talks, election forecasts, commercials for cars and soap. "And now," the anchorman announced, "a special report from our correspondent, Pat Burke."

"New Hampshire's most famous runaway has done it again," Pat began briskly. "Kate Prescott of Wingate has disappeared once more. This time, according to state and local police, she may have had some help. She took a ride on Old Winthrop Road about three o'clock Friday afternoon and has not been heard from since."

The picture moved from Pat Burke to the steps of the Wingate police station. Harry saw that Chief Torbert hadn't changed much. Lieutenant Sansone he recognized immediately from five years ago. He was one of the state policemen looking for Sharon. He hadn't found her, had he? Harry Bemis was encouraged. Down a step or two stood Kate's mother and sister, looking tired and embarrassed as usual. That other woman, the one with short gray hair, he hadn't seen her before. "Agatha Bates, a retired police officer from Boston," Torbert was saying.

Pat said something about kidnapping. The chief ducked the question. So did Sansone. The police always said they were making progress. That's all he heard for weeks after someone had carried Sharon off. Tomorrow's newspapers, he thought with satisfaction, would start carrying the story. He could finish the Kate Prescott scrapbook. Harry Bemis switched off the set and went back to work.

At ten-thirty, he heard Kate moving around upstairs. She tested the door handle. She used the bathroom. Harry looked out the study window. The patch of light from Kate's window disappeared from the ground outside. Good, kids need their sleep.

Pat Burke led off the news at eleven. As brisk as ever, Harry observed. Her hair and wardrobe were different. Almost breathless with impatience, she told Harry Bemis about a major breakthrough in the Kate Prescott case. She told him he had been watching Kate all summer from an abandoned trailer next to the Prescott house. She told him what he looked like. She told him he had parked across the road from the Wingate school. She told him he dressed like a businessman and probably traveled a lot in a black Buick. She even told him he ate French peppermints and was a litterbug. Finally she told him he could expect a visit from the police fairly soon.

Harry Bemis was startled, but the more he thought about it, the more he was convinced it was a bluff. It was just bits and pieces they fed to the news people. Pat hadn't told him his name. She hadn't told him where he lived. She didn't mention Margaret and Sharon. It was a bluff. It would take Torbert and his friends a couple of days to figure the rest out. If they wanted to poke around in an empty house, good luck to them. If they showed up on Wednesday they could help install the stove and refrigerator. Harry chuckled.

He went up to the bedroom. He picked up two suitcases and took them to the kitchen. He put them beside the door. How long had they been packed waiting for him, he wondered. When had he begun to make his plans? It was like trying to remember the details of a dream you never forgot but couldn't piece together. It wasn't so long ago. Was it last weekend sitting in the study that he decided, without ever admitting it, that he had to make Kate Prescott his daughter? It was all fuzzy now. That wasn't like him. Harry Bemis was famous in the company for never forgetting anything. That's why he was promoted to district sales manager.

Clothes for Kate. He took a suitcase from the front hall closet, one that Margaret had left behind. He emptied the boxes of new clothes into the suitcase, closed it, and put it beside his own.

What else, food? They wouldn't want to stop for a while. He filled a bag with cookies and junk food he had bought for Kate. Money? They'd go to the bank in Manchester early tomorrow. He'd close out the account. There was plenty there. Reports? The company could come and get them.

Was that everything? He turned out the lights in the kitchen and the study. Cautiously he went to the front door, eased it open, and listened. He heard only the wind through the pine trees and the loose shutter banging outside Margaret's room. Not a sound at the back door.

He stood there, indecisive, for a moment. You can never tell, he thought. It was better to be prepared. Sometimes plans didn't work out the way you wanted them to. That's why people bought insurance. You couldn't always tell. Harry Bemis went out to the garage. He returned with a plastic five-gallon can in each hand. He placed them beside the suitcases. "My insurance," he whispered, "just in case."

20

"What's he going to do, Agatha?" Torbert asked. They sat in the front of the Wingate police car, waiting for dawn. It was cold, almost bitter, in the car. Sansone had ordered the cars not to run their motors, although Chief Postma was certain they would not be heard in the Bemis house.

Agatha shrugged. "You tell me, Malcolm. You and Postma and Vincent know a lot more about Harry Bemis than I do. He must feel safe for a while. He didn't make a run for it last night, after the news."

"He must figure he has some time," Malcolm said.

"What was he doing out in the garage?" Agatha asked.

"Postma's men weren't close enough to see. They were told to wait and watch. That's what they did." Torbert peered at his watch. "It's five-thirty. The Prescotts will be here soon. Why did you and Vincent get them over here? This could be a nasty piece of business."

"Perhaps they can keep it from being nasty. Bemis knows them. He watched them all summer. He must have seen something of Lydia. She might be able to talk to him."

"How much talking do you think Sansone will put up with? He has his troops here. He's a tough officer, Agatha, I know for a fact. He goes by the book. He's not going to sit here all day waiting for Harry Bemis to come driving down the lane."

"I know that," Agatha remarked. "That's why I told him about Lieutenant Finnegan."

"Who's Lieutenant Finnegan?"

Agatha told Torbert about the adopted-child case. "When the father refused to give up his daughter and come out of the apartment, Finnegan decided to break in. I protested, but I was new on the job and they were going by the book. He and his partner hit the door together. There was a shot, then a terrible scream. They found the father in the bedroom, lying in a corner. The adopted daughter had her arms around him. She was out of her mind."

"That was pretty rough," Torbert commented.

"That's what Finnegan thought, too. He resigned after a couple of weeks and took up landscaping."

Vincent Sansone tapped on the window. He climbed into the backseat. "Looks like it's going to be a pretty good day. When the Prescotts arrive, I think we should move down the lane and announce ourselves. Postma agreed. He knows Bemis better than the rest of us. He doesn't expect any trouble. We're pretty sure Kate's okay. She must be up in the third floor where the light was on last night. Postma says there's a playroom up there. If Bemis balks, we'll let Lydia make a pitch for her daughter. After that, we'll see. All right with you, Malcolm?"

"It seems sensible. Agatha?"

"I'd like to try to talk to him first, Lieutenant. This isn't the same Harry Bemis Chief Postma knows. There's a kidnapped child between that man and the man down there in the house. He's living another life that we don't understand. He knows what he's going to do, I'm certain. We don't, so we better find out if we can. I'd like to go down and talk to him. Hold your people out of sight."

Malcolm protested. "You can't tell what the nut is going to do, Agatha."

"That's true, Malcolm, but a sixty-five-year-old woman isn't going to frighten him the way a bullhorn and cruisers with flashing lights are. It may not work. Let's see."

She opened the car door and headed for the lane. Sansone started to protest.

"Let her go, Vincent," Torbert said. "She's been an officer longer than we have. She knows what she's doing."

At six Harry Bemis awoke. He turned over on the old sofa in his study where he generally slept. A gray light sifted through the window. He rubbed his face with cold water in the kitchen. He put on his glasses and squinted out the back window. Nothing. In the half-dark he set the table and put a pan of water to heat on the hot plate.

On his way up to Kate's room he peered out of Margaret's window across the field. Nothing there, either. In the attic Kate was asleep deep under the covers, snoring lightly. She gave a start when Harry shook her shoulder. "Get up, Kate, and dress yourself. I'll wait outside. No lights, please."

He was tempted to turn on the television for the news at seven but, no, his plans were made. He followed Kate down to the kitchen.

"Why no lights, Mr. Atwood?" Kate asked.

"We blew a fuse, Kate. I don't want to make it any worse. I guess it doesn't matter. We're going to California as soon as we have our breakfast."

"California?" Kate woke up fast. California was all the way across the country. It was so far away they didn't even have the same time.

"Yes. We need a vacation, Kate. I haven't had one for almost six years, except for a week in Miami at a convention. You could use one, too. You didn't do anything exciting this summer as far as I could see."

"But California," Kate protested. She wouldn't stand a chance out there. "I can't leave Mom and Sandy just like that."

"Just eat your breakfast, Kate. We don't need to talk about it anymore. It's what I planned for us." He put an egg in the slotted spoon to drop into the boiling water.

There was a knock at the front door, a hard determined knock that echoed through the house. Kate half arose from her chair. Harry Bemis pushed her down firmly.

"Sit!" he ordered. "Don't you move, Kate. Don't you dare move. Not a sound." He reached over to the counter to turn the hot plate off.

A second knocking, harder and longer than the first. Harry Bemis crept down the hall into the shadows of the living room. There was no sign of a car in front of the house or down the lane. He was puzzled. The police wouldn't come banging on his door like this. He moved to the back of the door.

"What is it?" he asked in a thick voice.

21

Agatha Bates relaxed. Harry Bemis had come to the door. The rest was up to her.

"I'm with the police, Mr. Bemis. I'd like to come in and talk with you," she said as quietly as she dared. It was hard to know how well he could hear on the other side of a thick door.

It must be that woman, Harry Bemis thought. The friend of the Prescotts. What was her name? Agatha, Agatha Bates, that was it. Why would they send her? Did she come on her own? Hadn't she told Pat Burke she was just a friend? That was it. She *was* on her own. He would have seen the cars if the police were here. They were all over the place for days when Sharon disappeared. But how did she know who he was and where he lived? The police *must* know. What were they up to? Harry Bemis was confused.

"You must be mistaken," he answered. "My name is Atwood, Harry Atwood. This is the Atwood place. I'm afraid I don't know anyone named Bemis. They may live down the road. I just couldn't say. Now, if you'll excuse me, I'm cooking breakfast."

"Please don't go, Mr. Atwood," Agatha spoke louder. "I'm trying to locate a missing girl. Kate Prescott is her name. Ten years old. Curly light brown hair, freckles, about seventy pounds."

Harry Bemis smiled. Retired policewoman Bates *was* acting on her own. He and Kate were safe. "I can't help you. I haven't seen any kids along the road. I have to go look after my egg."

I'm going to lose him, Agatha thought. "Just a moment, Mr. Atwood. I notice you have a black Buick out back." Since it wasn't parked in front of the house, the car had to be in the back. "It has a bumper sticker, 'Insurance is the Best Policy.' That fits the description of the car that carried Kate Prescott off Friday afternoon. Did you lend your car to anyone Friday?"

"Of course not. I need my car for my work. I was up in North Conway on Friday. You must be mistaken. I don't know anything about insurance." Harry Bemis realized he was talking too much. He had to stay cool.

"If you'd ask me in, Mr. Atwood, I'm sure we could straighten it out. There must be a mistake somewhere. You see, the mailbox at the end of the lane has Bemis on it."

"Those were the people who lived here before us. I

forgot about them. We never bothered to change the box. I get my mail in town at the post office. I really have to go now. My egg will be hard-boiled."

"Mr. Bemis!" Agatha spoke as harshly as she could. "Mr. Bemis, listen to me. There are eight police cars at the end of your lane. There are some men there you already know, Chief Postma and Lieutenant Sansone from the state police. They're convinced you have kidnapped Kate Prescott. What am I going to tell them?"

"Tell them they have made a mistake," Harry shouted back. "Tell them to go away and leave me be. I didn't kidnap anybody. Kate wanted to come with me. She's asleep upstairs. Leave her be. Kids need their sleep. Tell Charlie Postma I'll come down to the station later on and talk to him. He'll understand."

"You should talk to me first, Mr. Bemis, so I can explain it to him and the others. Why don't you let me in? I'd like to see Kate, too."

"You're that woman, aren't you?" Harry Bemis said. "That Agatha Bates woman? I saw you on television yesterday. You said you had retired. I'm not going to talk to you. You have no right to be down here on my property. Get off or I'll file a complaint with Chief Postma."

"If I could only talk to Kate," Agatha answered, "she could tell me whether she wants to be here. I could then reassure her mother, you see. She's up there with Sandy, Kate's sister. You can imagine how worried they have been. You lost a child, Mr. Bemis. You know how helpless you feel. I'd like to reassure them. It's cold out here. I could use a cup of hot coffee. Let's talk it over inside."

It wasn't working out the way it should, Harry Bemis thought. The woman was trying to talk him out of the house. Maybe the police *were* out there waiting to take Kate away from him. They'd put him in a hospital, like Margaret. He knew he couldn't stand that.

"Look," he said to the door, "I can't let you in. You have a gun. That would frighten Kate. Tell Charlie to put away his guns and I'll bring Kate down to the station. She can talk to her mother and sister there. If she wants to go home with them, well, that's all right with me. We've had a good visit, and Kate could come back on weekends if she wants to. We're pretty good friends now, Kate and I. Tell the chief I'll be along in a couple of hours. Tell him he's made a mistake to think I'm a kidnapper, Lieutenant Bates. We can work it out."

Agatha reflected for a moment on Harry's offer. She understood she wasn't getting anywhere. Bemis wasn't about to let her into the house. It was equally certain he wasn't going to deliver Kate to the Madison police station. She doubted that he was going to make a run for it. Confused though he was, Harry Bemis knew that wouldn't work. Postma's men in back would have moved in closer to the Buick by now. But before she gave up, Agatha had to know Kate was alive.

"Could you bring Kate to the door, Mr. Bemis?" she suggested. "Then she could tell me herself she wants to stay here with you. I could tell her mother. Will you do that?"

"Just a moment, Lieutenant Bates. I'll go ask her. She must be awake by now what with all the shouting you've done."

He went back into the kitchen. Kate sat, white-faced and trembling, at the table. She hadn't moved, but she must have heard every word. "It's all right, Kate," he tried to reassure her. "We're still going to California. We'll stop and visit your mother and Sandy on the way." He picked up one of the red cans and carried it into the living room.

"She doesn't want to talk to you," he told Agatha. "She wants all of you to leave us alone. She agrees to see her mother later on. I can't do anything with her. She's afraid you'll take her away."

That was it. Agatha realized she had failed. Lieutenant Sansone and Chief Postma would take over now. "I'm sorry to hear that, Mr. Bemis. You know as well as I do the police aren't going to leave. I don't know what they will do, but you better prepare yourself to deal with them."

"I'm prepared, Lieutenant Bates," Bemis answered. He unscrewed the top of the plastic can. He poured gasoline over the floor and the carpets. He doused the furniture and the old piano Margaret had hated. He lifted the can to drench the bottom half of the heavy curtains. When the can was empty, he opened the door a crack.

"Can you smell the gasoline, Lieutenant Bates? I have

other cans in here with me. I will not talk anymore with you and your friends. If anyone comes close to this house, I will set it on fire. No one is going to separate Kate and me. That's all I have to say." He pushed the door shut and locked it.

22

"He means it, doesn't he?" Sansone asked Agatha.

"He means it. I could smell the gasoline all the way down to the lane. He must have soaked the room. He wasn't bluffing. That's what he was carrying in from the garage last night. He had this planned."

"After a while the gas will evaporate," Chief Postma said. "We'll just wait."

"It won't all evaporate. The living room will go up like a rocket. And he has more," Malcolm Torbert reminded him.

Lydia Prescott and Sandy stood on the edge of the discussion. "I told you he was insane," Lydia exclaimed with horror in her voice. "He should be put away for the rest of his life. How can he talk about burning Kate and himself up?"

"Perhaps if you talk to him over the horn, Mrs.

Prescott, he'll pay attention. We're not planning to do anything right now to upset him, you may be sure of that. But we can't let him stay in there forever either. We're going to move down the lane to a point where he can see us and hear us. Charlie, will you get all the fire equipment here you can round up? I'm going to put some more men in back. They may be able to get close enough to hit the back door."

Agatha spoke up. "I wouldn't try that, Vincent. You can be certain it's occurred to Bemis to barricade himself and Kate upstairs with his gasoline cans. You wouldn't reach them in time."

"We'll see, Lieutenant Bates," Sansone answered. "I will have to be responsible for the operation from now on."

The police cars, lights flashing, inched down the lane toward the house. Two hundred yards from the house they stopped and lined up across the lane and the edge of the field. Two officers with rifles leaned across the top of their cruisers, facing the house.

"Leave room for the fire trucks to get through," Sansone ordered. "All right, Mrs. Prescott, come over here and see what you can do."

Lydia followed Sansone to one of the cruisers where he handed her a bullhorn. She looked around. "Where is Sandy?" she asked. "Was she with you, Agatha?"

Agatha shook her head. There was no sign of Sandy. Malcolm Torbert checked the cars and talked to other officers. They all shook their heads. Sandy was nowhere to be seen.

* * *

Ducking behind the bushes and trees along the other side of the lane, Sandy made her way to the old stone house. She wasn't sure what she was going to do, but one thing was certain in her mind—she wasn't going to let that crazy man hurt her sister. The police seemed more interested in taking care of the Bemis guy than they were in helping Kate. All those guns frightened her. If she could just get inside, she'd think of something. She'd make Bemis listen to her.

Now she was opposite the house. She looked back. No one was close enough to stop her. She could dash across the lane up to the front door. They wouldn't dare come close when she was on the veranda. Bending over, she ran as fast as she could to the house.

She hit the door with furious fists. "Kate, Kate," she shouted. "Let me in, Kate."

The police heard her shouts. Two officers started toward the house. "Stop!" Agatha ordered.

The men straightened up and looked at Lieutenant Sansone. "We'll wait," he said. "Sandy will be safe enough, Mrs. Prescott," he said to Lydia. "Bemis isn't going to let her in."

Kate and Harry Bemis stared at each other across the kitchen table. A half-eaten doughnut lay on Kate's plate. How could he explain it all to Kate? Harry asked himself. How could he explain how important she was to him, that she belonged with him, no matter what? Why couldn't they leave him be until he had a chance to convince Kate she was better off with him looking after her than she was in a cheap mobile home with no father and only half a mother?

The silence was broken by a frenzied banging at the front door and a girl's voice shouting, "Kate, Kate, let me in."

Kate shot from her chair. She was halfway down the hallway before Bemis got to his feet. She slipped the chain, turned the lock, and then opened the door. Sandy stumbled into the room to Harry Bemis's feet. He reached around her to shut the door and lock it.

"What do you want here?" he demanded. "I told that Bates woman for all of you to stay away, or else."

"Kate is my sister," Sandy said defiantly. "You have no right to keep her here, I don't care what you say. Look at her, she's scared stiff. What have you done to Kate? Don't cry, Kate." Sandy took a red bandanna from her pocket and gave it to Kate.

"You better go," Harry Bemis said. "Go back and tell your mother that Kate has decided to stay with me. That's what I told Lieutenant Bates: Kate and I are going to stay here. If the police try to get in, the responsibility will be all theirs."

As she listened to the man who had stolen Kate away, an idea took shape in Sandy's head. "You say Kate wants to stay here with you?" she asked suspiciously.

"Of course she does. I'm not a kidnapper. I'm a friend of Kate's. Go on, Sandy, ask her. You want to stay here, don't you, Kate?"

Terrified and exhausted, Kate was unable to answer. She looked helplessly at Mr. Atwood, then Sandy.

"How's she going to answer with you standing over her like that?" Sandy asked Harry Bemis. "You stay out of it for a while. I'll talk to Kate alone. If that's what she wants, I'll go back and tell Mom and the others. Maybe they can straighten it out."

Before Bemis could open his mouth, Sandy led Kate down the hall toward the kitchen. Let her go, he thought. It can't do any harm. The back door was double locked. It was time he had faith in Kate. If he was going to be her father, he had to trust her. But if she wanted to leave, of course he couldn't permit that. He knew what was best for her. He stood in the middle of the living room breathing the gas fumes and waited.

Sandy and Kate returned sooner than he expected. Sandy hugged Kate hard and left her standing at the end of the living room. "Kate says she'll stay here for a while," she announced. "You're not a bad guy, I guess. Kate needs a father to look after her. She'll want to visit us regularly. I'll try to explain this to Mom. Is that what you want, Kate? Are you sure?"

Kate nodded. "Yes," she said softly.

"Let me out please, Mr. Atwood," Sandy asked.

Without a word, Harry Bemis undid the chain, turned the lock, and opened the door halfway for Sandy to leave.

A thunderbolt in jeans flashed across the room. It smashed into the back of Harry Bemis's legs. He lurched to his knees. Hands reached out to trap his arms and pull him across the doorway. Two bodies piled on top. Harry's glasses fell beyond his reach. He tried halfheartedly to rise, but his body was heavy and tired. Did he really want to get to his feet? he wondered. He had lost her now, lost her forever. He slumped to the floor, closed his eyes, and waited for the police and the people with the television cameras.

ABOUT THE AUTHOR

JAMES DUFFY is the author of a number of scholarly books on shipwrecks, slavery, and African history, and a novel for young readers, *The Revolt of the Teddy Bears*. He has received fellowships from the Bollingen Foundation, the Guggenheim Foundation, the Ford Foundation, and the Rockefeller Foundation. He lives in Arlington, Massachusetts.

Great FREE offer
just for you!

Join SNEAK PEEKS™!

Do you want to know what's new before anyone else? Do you like t
read great books about girls just like you? If you do, then you won
want to miss SNEAK PEEKS™! Be the first of your friends to know what
hot ... When you join SNEAK PEEKS™, we'll send you FREE insid
information in the mail about the latest books ... *before they'r*
published! Plus updates on your favorite series, authors, and excitin
new stories filled with friendship and fun ... adventure and mystery .
girlfriends and boyfriends.

It's easy to be a member of SNEAK PEEKS™. Just fill out the coupo
below ... and get ready for fun! It's FREE! Don't delay—sign up today

- -

Mail to: SNEAK PEEKS™,
        Bantam Books, P.O. Box 1011,
        South Holland, IL 60473

☐ YES! I want to be a member of Bantam's SNEAK PEEKS™ and receive hot-off-the-press information
in the mail.

Name _____ Birthdate _____
Address _____
City/State _____ Zip _____

SK31—6/89

- -